RING THE JUDAS BELL

by James Forman
THE SKIES OF CRETE
RING THE JUDAS BELL

RING
THE
JUDAS
BELL

• • • • • • • • • •

by James Forman

BELL BOOKS
Farrar, Straus & Giroux
NEW YORK

BELL BOOKS

is a division of Farrar, Straus and Giroux

For Kay, who labored long

1

It was early spring, and a boy in tattered homespun lay on a hillside surrounded by sheep. Nicholos Lanaras was happy; warmth stirred his limbs. High above, eagles hung on the air currents, and he watched reverently as though they were the children of Zeus. A sound distracted him. He turned, resting on his elbow, as it grew and attached itself to a distant speck. An airplane advanced steadily, and the eagles rose to meet it. During the Hitler war they had attacked the fighter planes, but this one had already outstripped the eagles. The sheep scattered and Nicholos, remembering what those other planes had done, ran for cover. He threw himself flat behind the overgrown columns of a Doric temple which an earthquake had leveled centuries before. The plane roared over. Recognizing the familiar star on the plane's tail, Nicholas stood up and waved eagerly, as though to atone for his distrust. The plane seemed to dip its wing. Nicholas guessed it was only from an upward surge of air, but it made him smile and wave again to the American plane which so swiftly passed down the valley of Serifos and out of his world.

With brandished staff Nicholos pursued his flock. One sleeve was shorter than the other, and his big knotty knees had worn through his trousers. Clothes hadn't mattered since his mother died, and the motion of his body was an adventure, like flying. He spread his arms, then caught his toe on a stone and nearly fell. This brought him back to a limping walk and the consideration of his sheep. Once there had been only wolves and gypsies to worry about, but now the countryside was full of wandering, starving people.

The Andarte were to blame, the mysterious night fighters who meant to overthrow the government or, failing that, to lay all Greece in ruins. Nicholos had never seen them, but he had seen the results of their work in the constant trickle of refugees fleeing south, so many and so pitiful that he had been drained of pity long ago.

Their suffering had become an overwhelming fact of life, their hunger a threat to his flock. The village of Serifos was filling up with those who could flee no further. Their mud huts spread chaotically about the granite geometry of the old town. Against these strangers Nicholos and the other shepherds defended their flocks as they did against wolves and bandits from the hills. They could not afford generosity. If all the sheep were slaughtered at once, all stomachs might be comfortably full for a few days, but with winter all would starve. The villagers themselves would have to join the hapless caravan on the road.

At first Nicholos had accompanied his father to the refugee camp and tried to help, but the camp grew rapidly and Serifos was poor. Nicholos stayed away finally, but the problem remained with him in the form of a ragged, limping little boy who had appeared one day in the pasture and returned again and again. Though Nicholos had made no

2

effort to befriend the child, he began to speculate on where he had come from, on why his right foot was so fearfully scarred. He came to accept the stranger as a fixture on the hillside until one morning, when his back was turned, the child made a dash at his smallest lamb, gathered it into his arms, and fled. As a crime it was a pitiful failure. The lamb outweighed the thief, and in a few strides Nicholos caught up. With fists as spare as sparrow's claws the child fought back. Nicholos bore him down, pinning his brittle wrists to the ground. The thief relaxed, conquered. His old-young face turned up to Nicholos, he awaited punishment with the expression of a creature inured to pain and determined to defend itself. Nicholos helped him up and told him to go and not return. And the child went, limping. "Oh God, does he have to limp?" Nicholos asked himself. He longed to call out to the boy, but a friendly sign would have been an invitation to future liberties. He silently watched the child out of sight and then drove his flock home, but even with his eyes wide open, fixed on the distant mountains, he could see those hollow eyes and the scarred foot.

Strangely, the child returned the following day. He seemed at first not to notice Nicholos, but sat down as though about to repeat his crime. Nicholos waited suspiciously until he caught a look of naked admiration so unmistakable that he had to resist an inclination to smile. It would be a mistake making friends with such a child, but it seemed even worse to sit and stare. He finally approached the stranger and asked his name.

"Christo," was the reply.

"What's wrong with your foot, Christo?" he asked— then, getting no response, added, "Have you a family?" Christo shook his head.

"Is it true that some mothers burned their children's feet so the Andarte wouldn't take them?"

"All the other children were taken," said Christo.

"You must be from Kotta. Almost everyone was killed there. Was your mother killed?"

"Yes."

"You remember her?"

"A little."

"I haven't a mother, either," said Nicholos. "Sometimes I dream about her, though."

"So do I. I dream of her chasing me with boiling water."

"Was it your father who told you to steal my sheep?"

Christo said he had no father. He had come alone with other refugees. They had taught him how to survive.

"Haven't you a father, either?" Christo asked.

"Oh, yes. My father's the priest. I'm to be priest one day."

"Do people ever come back?" the child asked.

"Of course, if they don't like the place they have gone."

"I don't mean that. I mean after they've been killed," said Christo.

"Nobody can do that," said Nicholos. "Nobody can come alive again."

"Jesus did."

Thus Nicholos, almost against his will, had accepted Christo. He shared his lunch that day with the boy, and continued to do so regularly, though he had grown out of the habit of making friends. Since his mother's execution he had distrusted involved contacts. When his sister Angela said, "I want people to know I'm alive. Don't you want them to know you're alive?" Nicholos could answer truthfully that he did not care. Of course he did not exclude his own family: his father, whom he loved with a kind of distant awe, and Angela. He loved her without reservation. Otherwise Nicholos gave himself primarily to his flock. For them he would risk his life, if need be, but people could betray him simply by dying.

His world was small, surrounded by mountains, and Nicholos could not help knowing its people as well as its geography. At the northern end of the valley the river Aliakon entered, flowing along like a serpent and vanishing again into an unknown universe. A rising gust of wind threw the village noises up to him. He could listen all day on the slopes and know what was going on below from the pounding, shouting, and slamming of doors.

The lonely mountains made the villagers noisy. When Dimitrov, the butcher, slaughtered a lamb, its terrible shrieks were music to their ears. In the evening would come shouts from the coffeehouse where older shepherds gathered to drink thick sweet coffee and make up fantastic lies. The air would reverberate as they shouted politics and damned the birds whose droppings from the mulberry tree fouled their tasseled caps and coffee trays. Nicholos would never be one of them. Sometimes this made him sad, but his future was a more responsible one. It belonged to the chapel and the Judas bell.

When the chapel bell rang, Nicholos knew other noises would cease. The chapel had stood for more than a thousand years. Half-buried by the great plane tree where owls hid from daytime hawks, it sparkled like a gem. Since the beadle had disappeared in the war, his father had taken over the chapel repairs, whitewashed it twice a year and restored the plaster. It was Father Lanaras, too, like a black ghost in the sunlight, who scoured the empty monks' cells and gave them sky-blue domes. One day Nicholos knew these tasks would fall to him.

This chapel where he would be priest had known over fifty generations of Christian priests, and before them pagan worshipers. Turkish bullets fired a century before had laid bare Doric columns. Nicholos had seen them, and he had seen the mosaic tile under the floor, which was Roman work. For Nicholos, for everyone in Serifos, the chapel was the center of life and death. When its bell spoke, they listened. It was ringing now, clear and emphatic, that ancient bell in whose metal was fused one of the thirty coins belonging to Judas Iscariot.

The bell rang urgently, summoning the congregation, and the boy was apprehensive, for it seemed once again to herald a great change. His life, the future of his family—of all Serifos—was deeply involved.

Always the bell's clanging had given a pattern to his life. When he was born the bell had rung. The good, innocent years had followed. Later, when Nicholos was still a child, its tolling had brought desperate, heartbreaking times.

He remembered the time of his innocence as a kind of sunshine Eden, all happiness. With his father he had pulled the great bell rope and his father had said, "There's no voice like a good bell. It's God calling us." They had rung in Easter week together, and Easter had meant feasting and song. His father had bowled stones with the other men, and he had won because his hands were large and square and capable as hands could be. Nicholos would never grow into his father's hands. His fingers were too long and delicate. Angela had said he must have stolen them from a saint.

After the feast his father had danced. While the beadle swung the censer in time, Father Lanaras leaped higher than

6

anyone else, his cassock streaming like wings, until his conical black hat rode down over his eyes. But most of all those innocent years had belonged to his mother.

She had gotten Father Lanaras to dance in the continental way, round and round, while the old people clapped and the shepherds sucked on their mustaches. His father no longer danced. No one did, and his mother was gone with all the happy things of Easter; with the rockets, the fireworks, and the furious hiss of the roasting ox.

The second time of his life, a time of heartbreak and prolonged desperation, also began with the voice of the Judas bell. This time his father had refused to pull the bell rope, for it meant the calling of volunteers. The mayor had rung it instead, and when the soldiers had marched through town Nicholos had laughed and cheered and pointed them out as though Angela and his mother were blind. They would push the macaroni-eaters into the sea. *"Nike! Nike!* Victory! Victory!"* he had shouted after the dusty men, but his mother had said softly, "Those poor boys. They're so young." His father had not watched the parade at all.

When winter ended, the victory would come with the help of God, said the radio, but when spring arrived they were fighting still. After the first Italian planes had come, Nicholos had helped dig a bomb shelter in the village square. Inside had been an altar and icons, and his father had stood beside them saying the prayers aloud in a steady voice when the bombers returned. Everyone else crouched on the floor while the earth beat and trembled like a sick heart.

Only afterward had Nicholos learned that the planes had not been Italian, but German. The Hitler war had begun. It had not seemed possible to Nicholos that soldiers from Serifos could lose, but before that day was over he knew that

7

they were coming home, silently, gaunt and shuffling on bandaged feet. "They aren't the same ones, are they?" Nicholos had asked, and Angela had taken him by the hand. They had gone inside where their mother was putting valuables into a box. That night Nicholos had seen the box buried under the floor.

With the thunderous roar of tanks pounding cobbles, the German army arrived before dawn. During the occupation the Judas bell rang for proclamations, restrictions, the taking of hostages, but it was never his father who pulled the cord. So far as Father Lanaras was concerned, Hitler was the Antichrist and he would rather be shot down like a dog than serve him.

With the other boys Nicholos had painted the great blue victory *V* on the walls, but the Germans had written under it, *Sieg ist unser*—"the victory is ours." Then they had sent three of the older boys to the concentration camp in Corinth. After that the Greek guerrillas, the Andarte, had blown up the power station and the chapel bell had rung for hostages. Thirty were taken, his mother among them, and when the Andarte did not surrender themselves to the Germans, the hostages were shot. Sometimes there returned to him a vision of his mother as he had last seen her, sweets upon her lips, coins sealing her eyes. Nicholos no longer wept for his mother. Once her memory had been all pain, like a screw boring into his flesh. Now the process was complete; the steel was safely lodged.

That was the winter of '44, third and last winter of the occupation, when nature and the Germans had seemed to compete in savagery. Nicholos would never forget the barefoot road gangs struggling through breast-high snowdrifts, and the she wolves coming down with their famished cubs to ravage the land. Now the wolves were returning, as though driven from their mountain haunts. Flocks had been mutilated and tracks had appeared near Serifos. They would not touch his sheep. This was a vow, for Nicholos felt as bound to his flock as his father was to his congregation.

In the spring of his twelfth year, Nicholos had become a shepherd. In the three years that had followed, he had watched the flock grow from five wasted beasts to the present throng. Not one animal had died or been lost through his fault. He loved each one, from Dassos, the great ram, to the tiniest lamb. He called each by name, names so foolishly endearing he never made them known even to Angela. Many shepherds carried rifles, but Nicholos, sighting down the barrel of his father's Mauser, had sensed that he could never drive a bullet into a living creature, even a wolf. Should the packs become bold enough to hunt during the day, he was prepared to meet them with bare hands and a courage that had never been tested.

His father had taken the Mauser rifle from the blackened carcass of a tank as the Germans retreated. He had emptied its magazine into the air. At last victory had rung from the chapel bell, calling the Andarte down from the hills to kiss the girls and the old women, and even the men. There had been joy in Serifos, but Nicholos had not liked the way they kissed Angela. He could never like the Andarte because his mother had died so they might live.

Thus the Hitler war had ended and Nicholos had expected his life to change. But there had been no change. The fighting went on and it was not solely because of wolves that shepherds carried weapons. It was because of the Andarte.

His father said war had robbed them of faith. Without faith, they had fallen in love with war and kept a secret army in the mountains. The schoolmaster said it was more complicated. It was politics. "You see, Nicholos," he had explained, "our government is a monarchy, but these Andarte are Communists. Other Communist countries like Albania send them supplies, and if they want more supplies they have to do what these Bolshevik countries tell them."

"*Bolshevik!*"

The name was evil. Nicholos thought of hob-nailed boots and little Russian princesses stabbed to death in their nightgowns. It was because of the Bolsheviks and the Andarte that the Judas bell was ringing now. Towns had been burned, and when a bomb had exploded in the old Turkish cemetery of Serifos there had been talk of posting sentinels and building barricades. According to his father, this would only provoke an attack. Men who fought chose the side of death, he said, and as spiritual leader he had to join the side of life, and life eternal. It was odd how his father used *Death* for so many things: war, evil, Satan himself.

One way or another the bell that was calling the people of Serifos to the chapel now would mean a third great change in Nicholos' life. Even now its peals were fading. His father must have gone to the altar, where the older men and women who had seen many wars would gather around him. The younger men, led by the schoolmaster, would oppose them. If they had their way and turned Serifos into an armed camp, Nicholos knew that his father would write an apology to the bishop and they would move. Move where? Though an Orthodox priest was permitted to marry as his father had done, marriage cost him all chance of promotion. Besides, so far as Nicholos was concerned, Serifos was the whole world.

Far below, the girls harvesting the premature wheat did not appear concerned. They went on with their work, while the young children charged through the cemetery, trampling the poppies and blue trumpetflowers, clambering over the German tank. They did not seem aware of the ringing bell or of the congregation moving toward the chapel. He envied their unconcern. Then one of the harvesters detached herself from the others, moved toward the slopes, and for a time he forgot the Judas bell. Though the figure was only a tiny dot in the distance, he immediately recognized the determined stride. As though leading a column of soldiers, Angela was coming toward the high pastures. For Nicholos she came like a victorious banner, blouse red for joy, short skirt whipping against her tanned knees.

She advanced on the playing children, feigning an attack, and their happy shouts came up to him. Nicholos smiled for those battles remembered at the cemetery wall, long before the tank had died there. However well he had fought, he had never won a battle or taken the wall. Always, until their last fight, the contest had ended with Angela's victory dance. She was two years older, good at fighting and wrestling to the point where her first defeat had come as a shock to them both. After that she had refused to play even when he had promised to lose.

Angela swung wide of the place where the tall pillared stones reared up. There hostages had been shot during the war. His mother had died on that spot, and part of his father, too. It was from that time that his father had begun using the words *Death* and *Satan* interchangeably, and ever since he had been coldly at war with this enemy. Little time remained for his two children, and Nicholas found himself imagining his mother's voice . . . downstairs . . . in another room . . . but it was always Angela's voice . . . Angela's voice

11

. . . until the two were overlaid and he could no longer remember the difference.

Angela was nearer now, springing on her heels, swinging her long arms, her head slightly down because of the grade. The Metaxas twins broke off their war game and leaped down from the German tank to follow her. The cobbler's daughter, Aphrodite, so frail and beautiful, with such long blonde hair that some said she must have nereid blood, took Angela's hand and skipped beside her. Angela could not help being liked. She had a face people could trust, and she had been his mother's favorite. Nicholos had always accepted this, and though Angela had qualities he would have disliked in others, he loved her more than any other human being. He loved her at the same time that he envied her way with people, her quick mind. There had been no schoolteacher during the war, but with their mother's help she had easily learned to read. She had tried to teach Nicholos after their mother was gone. His father had tried too, but Nicholos had no aptitude for written words. When he tried to put letters together, his head began to ache and he longed for the cool hills.

Nicholos recognized Angela as one who quietly dominated those about her. For years he had been her slave, until that last fight upon the wall. When he was tired or lonely, he regretted the process of growing up, for it was still easy to surrender unquestioningly to his sister.

She passed out of his vision finally, onto the steep hillside trail. He was used to it, but Angela was not. She would stop and rest below the last bend so that she would not appear tired when she arrived. Of course she would never admit it and he smiled to think of her sitting there.

Abruptly, two things occurred which extinguished his

private reflections. First he noticed a trail of dust on the valley road. Only a motor vehicle could raise such dust, and it was heading rapidly toward Serifos. The second distraction began vaguely with the clustering of his flock, as though an imperceptible jolt in the atmosphere's pressure had given them warning of a distant storm. The sky was clear. "It can't be wolves, not this time of day," he assured himself. "Wolves come only at night."

His words had scarcely faded when laughter convulsed the silence behind him. Nicholos whirled to confront the sound, his hands out from his sides. There stood a tall figure, lean as a winter wolf, tanned from harsh weather to a gypsy darkness. A turban bound back uncut hair and the stranger's face sprouted a scraggly young man's beard which gave an otherwise handsome face an air of corruption. To Nicholos he looked like a satyr, come to life from an ancient vase.

The mouth above the beard seemed to smile, though it might have been a trick of the shadows. Then the intruder advanced, brown snake boots murmuring through the grass. "*Cherete!* Glad to see an old friend," said the lips. The tone was noncommittal and suddenly Nicholos remembered the voice.

"Thanos Dimitrov! What are you doing here?"

"Well, you don't seem pleased to see an old friend."

"It's the way you came creeping up," said Nicholos.

He tried to hide his antipathy as Thanos sauntered toward him, swaying his head from side to side. His confident pace and the solid planting of his boots had something of the conqueror in them. Experienced, cocky and cruel, Thanos was a person Nicholos had once admired, then envied, and

13

finally loathed, though at times he still wished he could exchange his own bony face for the other's handsome one.

With a whinny of laughter, Thanos punched Nicholos on the shoulder. "Good to see you again. I mean that. Say, you're getting pretty big. Almost my size."

Taller, thought Nicholos, but he didn't say so.

Thanos offered him a lump of mastic gum. "I suspect you're curious about my brother. Well, Stavro's fine. He'd like to see you."

A year had passed since Stavro had disappeared with his older brother. His going had been a shock to Nicholos, one reason he did not trust new friendships. "I suppose he likes it up there," he said.

"Why shouldn't he? He's learning things. How to hunt. How to become a man. Remember the time the three of us hunted birds?"

"I'm not likely to forget it," said Nicholos. With a slingshot and a pouch full of lead balls, Thanos had led them to the olive grove. All he'd been able to hit was a nest full of fledglings in a hollow tree. He'd killed them all and stalked away while Nicholos and Stavro had stayed where they were, stunned. The mother bird had returned and disappeared inside the tree. Finally Nicholos had peered inside the crack. The mother was lying over her young, wings outspread, motionless, and, as Stavro had demonstrated with a twig, dead. Neither boy had ever returned to the grove. The Metaxas twins had taken their place on the hunting trips, and forever after Nicholos had understood one thing—that every living creature suffers pain—and he had silently promised himself that never again would he be a party to its infliction. He had thought that Stavro felt the same, until he had followed Thanos to the mountains.

14

"You don't have to stare. I'm not a ghost," said Thanos. "I was thinking about Stavro."

Actually Nicholos was trying to decide what had happened to change the other's face. It wasn't the new beard, or the hair, twisted about his forehead in peaks, that made his face look mad. It was the eyes. They had always been strange, as though into each pupil a drop of milk had been infused. Something about the eyes had changed.

"You like guns? Look, here's a beauty." Thanos unlimbered a rifle from his shoulder. "Up there anyone can have one." This sounded like an invitation, and Nicholos recalled Thanos and his first gun. Until then there had always been welts on the boy's back, the width of his father's leather belt. But after Thanos had appeared with the gun, there had been no more beatings. The neighbors had expected the gun to go off one night, but for several years they were disappointed. Finally, both brothers had vanished.

Nicholos said, "You shouldn't be here, you know."

"No? I have a family in that town. There's nothing wrong in my visiting my old father and mother, is there?"

If he thought he was convincing anyone, he was a fool. Nicholos knew better. Behind the impassive face there was some intelligence. Nicholos could not guess the intention, but of one thing he was sure. Thanos was deadly. It was in his eyes. He was a killer, and Nicholos was very anxious to have him out of the way before Angela appeared.

"You're one of them. That's right, isn't it?"

"Who are you talking about? Why don't you say what you mean?" replied Thanos, and a hand settled between Nicholos' shoulder blades, heavier this time.

"I mean you're one of the Andarte."

To this Nicholos received no response beyond a slow

lipless smile in which the eyes played no part. No answer was required. The household had been a noisy one. Nicholos had heard the thunderous disputes between a royalist father and a son who needed to hurt back. If the devil himself were recruiting troops to overthrow the King, Nicholos could not entirely blame Thanos for marching beside him.

"Well, if you aren't, you won't care that the Gendarmes have been here."

"Gendarmes!" Hands tightened on the rifle until the fingernails went purple and white.

Observing the wedge, Nicholos sought to drive it wider with a lie. "And they're after you." He was in a reckless frame of mind. Angela was resting just below the meadow. In a moment she would come over the ridge.

"After me? . . . Personally? . . . That's a damned lie."

Nicholos had committed himself to a verbal precipice. There was no turning back. "Yes, there are posters about you."

"You're a liar!"

"Look, you can see their truck. It's in Serifos."

"Unless my father . . . he might." The implication did not come. "Admit you're lying."

"Go away."

"Admit about the posters."

Nicholos felt fingers on the back of his neck. They did not tighten but he could tell the nails were very long. His own were short, bitten down to the verge of drawing blood.

Nicholos sat down on a boulder. Shepherd life had made him tough as whipcord, and he was quick. It was only his father's teaching that kept him from hurling a stone at Thanos. Even the gun would not have stopped him.

"There isn't any sense quarreling, not when we have so

much in common," said Thanos, by which Nicholos supposed he meant Angela. "We're comrades, aren't we? Admit it." Nicholos kept silent. There came another slap on his shoulder, and this time it was painful. A quick pulse beat in Nicholos' wrist. He was big enough, all right. At this moment he would have liked to look tough, with a purple scar or a stubbly chin, but his attempts at framing a fierce expression before his mirror had always failed. The bones of his face looked brittle, and his black eyes reflected at most stern disbelief, more often surprise and bafflement.

"Get out of here," said Nicholos. His voice was terribly controlled and high. "If you don't leave—" But he wasn't going to fight. He didn't believe in fighting and besides he had no weapon and the hand still rested heavily on his shoulder while the voice said, dry and hard, "Little shepherd, what's wrong with you? Haven't I been friendly with you? I'd like to be your friend. I don't want us anything but friends when Angela comes."

So it was a rendezvous. That the two of them might have planned a meeting had not occurred to Nicholos before. The realization took all resistance out of him.

At this moment Angela came into view. She gave a little cry and began to run. Thanos waved with one hand; Nicholos felt the other still at the back of his neck. Before Thanos strolled jauntily off to meet Angela, his long nails dug into Nicholos' flesh.

Angela arrived, panting. "Oh, that was a climb." Her voice had a musical quality. Sometimes it dropped as low as a boy's, and Nicholos would remember her standing on the cemetery wall. "I don't know what the two of you see in these mountains." It was true that Nicholos loved the mountains. They were dependable on their own terms. They did not

17

die quickly, and they were more real to him than his father's sermons. There were no mountains in all the world as high as he could wish, for on the heights he could be alone and at peace.

Angela addressed them jointly as though they actually were friends in conspiracy. Nicholos did not look up at first, not wanting to see them together. He saw only Angela's legs planted there, long and brown and crisscrossed with the scars of thorns and thistles. Then she began questioning him and his eyes rose to her square thin shoulders and the strong features which reminded him of heroic sculptures. Set in this face were eyes so black and steady and unchildlike, so like his mother's eyes, that he could not always look into them. Her careless hair, dark and wild like his own, shone in the sun like a black bird's wing.

"Nicholos, what's wrong with you?" she asked. "You're acting queer. Have you been fighting?"

He replied with a locked jaw as if silently to say he knew what was going on and there was no need for her to disguise it.

"Tell me, Nicholos, what's happened? Has he done anything to you?" Her black eyes stared into his, direct and searching. "I don't like the way you're sitting, hunched up like that."

"That's not the point, though, is it? You didn't come all the way up here because of the way I'm sitting. . . . In case you haven't noticed, there's someone to see you." His own words annoyed him, they were so petty and useless.

"I don't think he likes his sister having friends," said Thanos.

The girl ran one index finger along Nicholos' coat sleeve.

18

"I didn't want to meet him here, Nicholos, but there wasn't any other place."

"We can go somewhere else if we're bothering him," said Thanos.

"You didn't risk your neck to pester Nicholos," replied Angela.

"True. . . . I came for news—and to flirt with you."

"All you'll get is news," she told him. Then, smiling brilliantly, "For a price, that is."

"Go on."

"You used to pass out cigarettes to the older girls."

"Cigarettes are hard to get," said Thanos, but he produced a couple from his pocket. Angela took one and he tossed her the matches. She didn't get a light and laughingly Thanos retrieved the cigarette and lit it. "These things are bad for little girls . . . unless they're bad little girls," he said. Then he put the cigarette between Angela's lips.

The intimacy of the gesture both enraged and chilled Nicholos. "Angela, don't," he pleaded.

"See if you can get rid of that shepherd. Tell him his sheep are getting lost," said Thanos. His manner was bored and he opened his mouth in a yawn. His lips assumed a strangely voracious aspect, as though he meant to swallow the human race.

"If you go on teasing, you won't get any news," said Angela.

"Yes I will," said Thanos, "because I'm your hero and you'd like to be my girl."

"Is that so?" said Angela. To Nicholos she seemed annoyed, but it might only be a pose for his benefit.

"Go away, Nicholos. You're embarrassing your sister. . . . No? If you're not leaving, I suppose we'll have to go . . .

19

that'd be much better, really. When a person grows up, there's not much using hanging around here. One can hardly breathe in plod-along Serifos, isn't that so? You know there're plenty of girls with us in the mountains, finding out there's more to life than cooking and keeping house. Serifos isn't a bad place for burying old people, but I don't think you belong here any more, Angela. What do you say? Up there, it's a new life." He repeated the phrase. "Think of it, a new life."

"It won't do, that's all, and would you like to know why?" said Angela.

"No."

"I'll tell you anyway. You're just a little bit too crazy. But there is one thing I like about you. You've got the most aristocratic ears. I think you ought to wear a huge gold ring."

"You don't know what you're missing. We've been living in a cave. Like one of those Italian cathedrals you're always talking about." He dropped his information casually, like a secret too old to keep.

"If you'd like, I could pierce the ear myself," said Angela.

"It's not far from here. Have a look. Might change your mind. We won't be there long," he admitted. "I hear the Gendarmes are in town."

"I think you're afraid of its hurting. It doesn't, though. Just a tiny prick."

Nicholos listened, drawing no amusement from this game of words. He was concerned for Angela with an animal loyalty stronger than his Christian conscience. In his hand a rock lay concealed.

Evidently the Andarte, too, had tired of the game, for as Nicholos listened, his tone changed. When Angela went on about the ears, he simply talked louder than she did. He shouted. "Your brother tells me the Gendarmes have been looking for me."

"Soldiers, not the police," she said. "I understand they will be massing down the valley."

"When?"

"Tomorrow, maybe the day after."

"Why didn't you say so?"

"I just did say so, and you'd better let me finish. They'll be coming up with trucks and cannon to comb the hills."

Thanos seemed suddenly to crumple in on himself. "I'm tired of running away," he mumbled. Then to Angela, "Well, thanks anyway. We'll have to walk all night. You won't change your mind . . . about coming?"

"If you were going to Rome or Paris, I might think about it," said Angela. "But mountains? You can keep them to yourself."

"I could force you, if I wanted," said Thanos in a weary voice, without the least bit of force supporting it.

A quick touch of electricity seemed to strike Nicholos. His knuckles grew white and the stone was hard in his hand.

"I'd claw your eyes out first," Angela said in a clear cool voice.

Nicholos believed her quite literally. Her slim legs were firmly planted and her posture was ramrod straight. But he could not help wondering what might have happened if he had not been present. Perhaps Angela had chosen this place as a restraint upon Thanos, or, a more disturbing possibility, as a restraint upon herself.

"Well, you're smart," said Thanos. "I can tell you all about caves and mountains, but if I had a decent home, I'd go there. You wouldn't catch me up here again."

"Your father'd take you back," said Nicholos.

"He'd kill me . . . or I'd kill him. . . ." And here the brief crack in the Andarte's armor sealed itself. He took a deep breath. "All right, I'm off. I'd like some information on what's going on. You know where and when." This was not said to Nicholos, but it was not presented as a secret from him either. With a hand on Angela's shoulder, Thanos tried to kiss her, but she held herself back. Immediately he appeared to lose interest, adjusted his rifle, and turned away. Before Nicholos he paused. "Good-by, little shepherd. Don't hate me too much. Shall I give Stavro your regards?" He smiled a wolfish smile. "All right, as long as you insist. Maybe I can arrange for him to come home. He's too young for this life."

Nicholos did not answer. He was too confused. At one moment he had wanted to see Thanos at his feet, a stone crushing his skull. And now? Now he didn't know. He wanted to tell Thanos he was sorry, but the Andarte was already strolling away. His voice floated back, singing the old ballad "The Vlach Shepherd," which Nicholos had heard at the coffeehouse, but never in the presence of women. The voice diminished, as the figure seemed to move more swiftly, more surely, like a beast that approaches its home earth. Then Thanos was gone, while Nicholos wondered silently whether he had misjudged the Andarte. No, Thanos was a killer and should be destroyed, not with hatred or jealousy, but with the same sense of necessity with which a doctor attacked a plague.

Brother and sister stood alone among the sheep. Above them, in the direction Thanos had taken, clouds were building above the sinewy peaks. Angela observed that it would rain, but Nicholos refused to be diverted. Useless as they might be, his thoughts had to be spoken.

"Angela, have you any idea what you've done? With Father down there, trying to keep Serifos from war, you've been spying for the Andarte. Spying! If anyone should find out!"

As though to bring their father more directly into the scene, there came a noisy exodus from the chapel far below. The meeting was over, though Angela seemed not to notice. "It isn't like that," she told him. "You know Thanos has always been a friend. He's had a rotten life. I'm sorry for him, and all I did was tell him about the soldiers so that he won't be taken and killed. Father would have done that. He's always talking about saving life. Why else did he hold the meeting today?"

Embattled, her expression was that of a young tigress. As Nicholos well knew, the more wrong she felt, the more Angela's arguments became insistent, logical.

"You ordinarily make fun of what Father says," replied Nicholos. When Angela accused their father of caring more for his ideals than for his children, Nicholos felt a pang of truth. At first, when his mother was gone and the world had seemed drowning and empty, he had turned to his father, but instead of solace he had received instruction, patient and cold. Gradually he had realized that his father was alone too. They never spoke of the dead or of the old days, but of religious things and ideals of human conduct. When Angela satirized their father's principles, Nicholos could not sympathize. He was entirely imbued with his father's fierce spirit of dedication. "To receive the call," his father had told him, "is the greatest honor that God can bestow." This Nicholos acknowledged, though he could not imagine ever taking his father's place or ever moving as close to God. But Angela would say, "I wish he'd move a bit closer to us." Nicholos had never found a reply he could trust.

"Perhaps I'm not in love with all humanity," Angela said, "but I believe in helping myself and my friends. Please, let's not talk about it any more. That's how I feel and there isn't any use arguing about it. Let's forget Thanos."

"If you're going home now, I'll go with you. Give me a hand collecting the flock."

This took only a moment. The sheep had already gathered themselves into a rippling cluster of curly backs and black faces. He said, "They can feel the storm coming, and so can I." Angela had told him all about storms; about warm moist air, cold currents, pressure systems. She confronted nature with knowledge; Nicholos felt the weather in his bones.

Angela drew his arm through her own, but it was not easy to walk that way on the narrow path and he could not say what he had to with their arms linked. He soon pulled away. They walked for a moment in silence, listening to the valley. As the shadows rose, it looked like the inside of a ship filling with black water. Finally he said, "Angela, I can understand not wanting him killed, but why do you have to follow him around the way you do?"

"I don't."

"You used to."

"Well, he's changed."

"He's the same," said Nicholos.

"Then it's me. I've changed."

"Angela, do you remember how we used to talk? We never used to hold anything back. We'd talk for hours, remember?"

Angela turned to him with sudden warmth. "You're still my favorite person. I guess you know that. And Nicholos, whatever I do, I never lie to you. But I'm older than you are, and I don't think you have any idea how different things are for a girl."

"I'd only like to understand this business with Thanos."

"I would too," she said. "I like him, and I don't know why. Maybe it's because he does exciting things. Even if what he does is wrong, it's exciting."

"You'd like being a man, wouldn't you?"

There was no need for an answer. He supposed it was the wish of many women, so many it had gotten into a story about the girl who went to war and fought so hard she turned into a man. He had teased Angela with this before.

"You can put it that way, if you want, but it isn't just being a man. It's having a man's opportunities. Have you any idea what it's like being a woman in Serifos? It's as if every day a huge monster nibbles away at you, just a little every day, and finally you'll be inside that monster and never be able to get out."

"I know, you'd like to see Paris or Rome, like Mother. But life isn't all a holiday, Angela."

"It ought to be. It really ought to be," she said. "I'm not saying Thanos is perfect. Sometimes I know he's awful. That's why I flirt with him all the time. If I tried taking him seriously, I'd end up telling him what an ass he is. Still, he's handsome. He has such piercing eyes."

"That's another thing," said Nicholos. "There's something queer about one of his eyes."

"Yes, he was almost killed. A bullet grazed the eyebrow and left a scar. . . . Don't look so troubled, Nicholos. It isn't your worry. . . . Your hand's a fist. Give it to me." Her

25

fingers curled lightly around his, a touch cool as ivory. She gave his hand a squeeze. "You're so good, Nicholas. Sometimes I'm a little afraid of you. Even with your great knobbly knees sticking out, you're so like Father. In all my life I've never been afraid of anything, except Father and his goodness. Because sometimes I'm bound to disappoint him, and you too. There is one thing you can do if you don't want Father hurt. Don't tell him about Thanos. He'd just be upset, you know. Promise you won't tell."

"I won't tell anyone," said Nicholos.

All at once her look of concern fell away. In its stead flowered a smile of such extraordinary warmth that her face seemed to Nicholas the most beautiful face he had ever seen; not Angela's face at all, but the lovely face from his childhood. In return, he gave her a bright false smile. Something unsaid, perhaps unsayable, remained between them. But the only arguments left to him were his father's: cold, without comfort, demanding more than people could ordinarily give. To speak now with his father's words would annoy her, yet to keep silent, as he chose to do, seemed the postponing of unhappiness.

They had descended the path and arrived at the first stony fields. A bat, like a black glove, whirled past, and all at once Nicholos was aware of evening as the end of warmth and sunshine. From the casting shadows of the Judas trees, darkness flowed toward Serifos. The storm was very near.

"All right, you two! Stop right there!"

It was a national guardsman, a short round individual who rose smartly to the tips of his boots, returning to his heels with a sharp cracking of a little leather riding crop against his puttees. "You both will have to answer some questions. Sergeant!"

Angela seemed terribly calm. "Will this take long?" she said.

"As long as it has to. . . . Sergeant, see to the boy!"

The sergeant was young, with a friendly adolescent face which was trying to frown. "I'll have to search you," he said to Nicholos.

"What will he do with my sister?"

"The Captain will question her. Don't worry, as long as you answer truthfully. If you don't mind, I'll have to search you for weapons."

Nicholos didn't mind at all. It was a game and he was delighted to be searched. "Is this an ambush? Have you been waiting for us?"

"I wouldn't call it an ambush," said the sergeant. "But if it is one, you can't escape unless you cooperate."

"I will."

"Who were you with up there?"

"My sister."

"Besides your sister."

Nicholos did not trust himself to answer. He had promised Angela, but he was a poor liar. The best Nicholos could do was stare silently into the sergeant's eyes.

"Who else was there?"

"My sheep."

The sergeant rolled a match from one side of his mouth to the other. "Listen," he said, "we saw three of you through binoculars. The other one vanished. Now what would you say you were doing with that person?" The sergeant began to look as though his uniform was uncomfortable. Regretfully he explained, "I've been ordered to use force if need be. It will be painful."

But Nicholos did not fear physical hurt. He had always

lived a little apart from his body, regarding it as no more than a house for his spirit, and during the war years that house had suffered hunger and cold, the slashing jaws of a wolf. Besides, he had pledged his word, and to preserve that pledge he was willing to endure pain until consciousness failed.

"I'm really sorry about this," said the sergeant, preparing to do something to Nicholos' arm which he had already twisted behind his back. Then, as Nicholos tried to shut himself off with the lines his mother had taught him, "Oh lamb of God, grant us thy peace, Oh lamb . . ." the captain interrupted.

"That won't be necessary, Sergeant. The girl has cleared things up. They can go home."

The sergeant and Nicholos breathed a mutual sigh of relief. As if anxious to bridge the unhappy gap between them, he stuck out his hand to Nicholos, saying, "All will be well one day."

Nicholos did not realize immediately the enormity of Angela's betrayal, and it was not until they were alone and passing the cemetery that he challenged her. "Why? Why did you tell? I don't understand you, Angela. I thought you cared for him." It seemed to Nicholos his sister was a stranger whose acts he could not predict.

"What would you expect? Did you think I'd let myself be beaten for no reason?"

"I would have," said Nicholos. "You asked me not to tell."

"I asked you not to tell Father. I didn't say anything about soldiers. I said it was an Andarte, and that he had us covered with a gun and that he ordered us to tell everything we knew, but that we didn't know anything anyway. Then he went away. That's all."

"But now they know the Andarte are up there."

"Naturally. They knew that anyway; everyone does. Besides, I found out when the rest of the soldiers are coming. They'll be here by morning."

"Do you plan to tell the Andarte about them?"

"I'll tell Thanos if I can. Then the Andarte will run away. No one will be hurt, and if there's no fighting the villagers won't want to arm themselves."

This seemed sensible, though somewhere Nicholos sensed a flaw; not in the plan's practicality, but in its morality. It was Angela's nature to assemble the facts quickly, too quickly. Never did she give herself time to reflect, but devoured one book after another, so rapidly their father had once asked the doctor if there was any danger of her going blind.

Nicholos had often asked her why she read that way. Angela had replied, "Because I'm afraid of what I don't understand." He had supposed she must be afraid of a great many things.

He himself lived peacefully with ignorance, and now he imagined Angela had passed beyond fear. There seemed little more for her to learn from books. If only she would give him time, there was so much he would like to tell her about sheep, about mountains, about what he thought was good and bad. When he tried, she made fun of his ideas by quoting things she had read which he could not understand.

Nicholos used to imagine that one day he would automatically inherit her ability and certainty of objective. Now he secretly sensed this would never be, simply because she was quick-witted and he was not.

"Am I letting you down again? I have a feeling you'd never let me down, Nicholos. . . . You have such trust in your eyes. I hope you never lose it."

They had reached the stone corral in the thickening rain. The sheep swept in while Nicholos counted them. One was missing, the smallest, the one that had been sick. He did not mind the rain or the dark, but his stomach was already rumbling as it always did before dinner. Still, it was little Ajax, his favorite because he had saved its life once before. Now he had no doubt that he must go back.

"You can't do that. Don't be a stubborn fool. It's pitch dark, Nicholos, and it's raining hard. In the mountains you'll fall and get hurt."

He could not let her arguments undermine his resolve. "I have to go," he told her, "or Ajax will die."

"Ajax? You'll be shot for an Andarte."

This stopped him. The Andarte might still be there, the militia too, probing through the darkness for one another. Angela had him by the arm, coaxing and pulling. He let himself be pulled, but all his instincts were in rebellion.

"Now you're acting like a sane human being, Nicholos. I hate to be nagging all the time, but honestly, you don't always use your head. What's one sheep, anyway?"

He did not answer. One sheep was meat and wool against hunger and cold, but he didn't think of Ajax that way. He had never lost a sheep, and he was picturing the storm-driven lamb with wolves abroad, and men like wolves.

Through the town they went side by side, heads bowed against the downpour. On the whitewashed walls signs were carelessly painted. WE WILL SHED BLOOD splashed in huge letters by the hand of an Andarte in the dead of night. Another hand had scratched through the letters with a chisel.

Beside it a new sign in drizzling red announced PREPARE FOR DEATH, THE ANDARTE WILL EAT WOOD. Such slogans had become commonplace, and neither one noticed them in their haste to be home. Together the rain and the red paint ran down, blurring the letters, mingling the signs.

2

Nicholos held the door open wide, for Roberto Bellofatto was a wide man. Built like a bear and with a gait to match, the Italian schoolteacher shambled toward the Lanaras house through the rain. Nicholos had grown fond of this one-time foe. His father liked Roberto too, though the Italian argued before his congregation all those views which Father Lanaras rejected.

"Health and joy!" said Roberto with his hand raised in a popish gesture. He limped to the center of the monastic little room and planted himself on a stool. "It's the Flood, Nicholos. God has finally reconsidered." Water gave a sheen to his blue jowls. It fell from his woolen cloak, forming a pool, and Nicholos might have laughed were it not for his lamb, and what the rain would be doing to it. Why did it have to be Ajax, the one born out of season that he bottle-fed through the winter?

"They're having a time down at the Modesty," said Roberto, referring to the café which in better times had been a butcher shop as well. "If your father and I accomplish nothing else, we keep Serifos from dying of boredom."

"I hear nothing came of the meeting today," said Nicholos.

"The Gendarmes broke it up. Now we're waiting to see what the soldiers will do," said Roberto, pulling a tobacco pouch from his belt and beginning to roll a cigarette. "But some of us aren't satisfied. Nicholos, your father is too generous with people. He's like a rooster trying to lay eggs. One day he's going to be asked for something he can't afford to give away, but he won't know how to refuse." Nicholos laughed at this. He thought Roberto was funny with his bright bow tie and his little black mustache which looked painted on his face with a very fine brush. Rarely could he take Roberto seriously, though it was otherwise with his father. Nicholos could not often laugh at the things his father thought were amusing.

"I mean that," said Roberto. "He didn't have to bring me back from prison camp to die in his home, and then feed me so well that I recovered. If he were an ordinary man, he'd regret that, now that I seem to be standing in his way. . . . I don't know . . . you would think I'd be grateful enough to keep silent, this one time, but I've grown fond of Serifos. I want to teach here for a while, and I want children in the school to teach."

With his father, Nicholos had been to the opening of the prison camp. He had borne Roberto's weight on his shoulder when they had brought him home. Frostbite cost the Italian six toes and his first lurching walks about Serifos were haunted by children singing "Mussolini the Buffoon." But Roberto had sung along with them and had made them laugh. Now fully recovered, he was a fixture in Serifos. At first he had talked of returning to a wife in Assisi, until a letter came saying that she had remarried. "Women!" Roberto had said, tapping a gland in his neck. "An old husband is like old furniture—to be replaced." Then he had talked of going home to create a scandal, but finally he had written a letter, signed by a friend, reporting his own heroic death.

"Yes, and here I am buried," he would say. In the three years that had passed, Nicholos had come to know him, perhaps, better than he knew his own father. On the surface Roberto was a talker, an easygoing, jabbering man who laughed at himself and everyone else. He had served with the Alpine division that the Evzones had routed at Metsofov. "*Aera! Aera!*" he would imitate the Greek war cry, and clap his hands over his head. Nicholos never tired of his tales.

When Italy collapsed Roberto had found himself first in a German, then in a Greek prison camp. "A place where reluctant soldiers are promoted back into civilian life" was how Roberto put it. But Nicholos had been there. Such camps were really cemeteries for the living. Remembering this, and sensing how dreadful Roberto's memories must be, it seemed impossible that Roberto could talk of arming Serifos. But he did talk of it, and many of the villagers supported him. Did he wish to invite war back again? Clearly, Roberto was no fool. Father Lanaras had been sufficiently impressed with his intelligence to sponsor him for school-teacher over the objections of those who suspected a foreigner.

"Nicholos, I don't want everyone in this household believing I'm a warmonger. I'm not."

"You know what I think," said Nicholos.

"Fine. You agree with your father, and you have his broad sin-bearing shoulders, too. That's how it should be with a son. This may surprise you, coming from a sinner, but

I agree with you both, in theory. What a wonderful world without any war, but we don't seem ready yet."

"Someone has to make a start," said Nicholos.

"Don't misunderstand me, as your father does. I'm not telling the villagers to fight. I'm simply trying to get them to arm themselves, to be prepared in case the Andarte come."

"Father says that's the first step toward fighting," said Nicholos, who was no longer enjoying himself. Laughter was what he wanted from Roberto, but the round little man seemed deadly serious.

"Perhaps, but there is one thing your father refuses to understand. We have some Zervas partisans in this town. That Dimitrov. . . . You'd think he was Kolokotrones at least. . . . 'God has taught us how to behave to anti-Christian Communists who have sold their souls to the devil.' That's what he's shouting. Believe me, it isn't funny. If we could only get them to let off steam by building a few barricades, doing sentry duty. I wonder if your father can understand that? With a little wine inside me, I'll probably tell him he's the best and most foolish man in the world. We're wasting precious time. War looks down on us like a hungry wolf, it licks its chops, while we. . . . Listen, this afternoon the militia arrived."

"I know," said Nicholos.

"Not about the proclamation on the tavern door, I imagine. You should see everyone down there with their lips moving, trying to read it. They'll have us in this war whether your father likes it or not."

"What does it say?"

"Something about a new constitution and about those of us who encourage the Andarte going to prison. I didn't read it all. When the shooting started, we ducked inside."

"Did you say there was shooting?"

This question came from Angela, who had appeared from the darkness of an inner doorway. In her hands was a long-necked purple vase, and her hands were so tight about its slender neck that she seemed to be strangling it.

"They say in the tavern that the Gendarmes stumbled across some Andarte, but after a few shots they were so frightened they ran away to wait for the soldiers."

"Was anyone killed?"

"Oh, they say an Andarte was hit. I don't believe it," said Roberto. "Such rotten shots. But that's nothing to you or me on a rainy night. . . . And where's the master of the house?"

"He's been out. He's getting into dry clothes," said Nicholos.

"You don't know who it was?" asked Angela.

"Who are you talking about?"

"The one they say was shot."

"No idea," said Roberto.

Nicholos knew she wanted to find out more, but with the sound of their father approaching Angela began pouring oil from the vase into the lamps. She could pretend all she liked, but her mind was outside—as his was. If he had a chance he would tell her about the proclamation. Then perhaps she would stay home tonight.

"Ah, the master of the house at last," said Roberto, standing up and taking one rolling step toward Father Lanaras. "Once again I'm taking advantage of your hospitality in hard times."

"As long as I'm here, there will be a place set for you," said Father Lanaras. There was regularly a fourth service at the table. If Roberto was not filling it, little Christo was,

36

and if there was not enough food for all, it was Father Lanaras who said he was not hungry.

Once Nicholos had overheard a stranger say of his father, "Look at the size of him. There is a priest who will make God jealous." Until then Nicholos had not been conscious of his father's unusual height, but Father Lanaras was so tall he made his chapel seem small. Nicholos knew too that under his dark vestments, his father's frame was a coil of muscle, which terrible self-control seldom revealed. Some said their father looked like Christ. The fine beard was as black as a funeral plume, but the chiseled features had been darkened by the years and by hard weather and Nicholos saw in his father's eyes a violence that was never Christ's. He recognized in his father an inner conflict which could have belonged to Jesus only for a moment, when the nails were being driven home.

"Look here," said Roberto. "I've brought something to show you." He produced a letter from inside his jacket. Each of the corners was charred.

"It's a warning," said Father Lanaras. "Presently you will receive one of these," and from a shelf he took an envelope, and shook from it a black paper dagger and a straight-razor blade.

"Good God! They dared send one of those to a priest!" exclaimed Roberto. "Who would do such a thing?"

"My dear friend, I would not even want to know."

Nicholos had seen the letter before. It still shocked him that his father should have received a death threat, and it was no comfort that his father ignored it. A storm was rolling toward them all. A thunderbolt seemed poised and aimed.

Angela returned to the room with a tray of food which she set upon the low table. So far as Nicholos could tell from her manner, the affairs of the outer night did not concern her.

Roberto announced generously, "It's a scene from Balthazar's feast!" Father Lanaras said grace, gazing across the table at a particular spot on the wall where Nicholos presumed God to be. The others sat with bowed heads until Father Lanaras expelled his breath in a long sigh. Then Angela poured four glasses of water from an enormous pitcher. Roberto made smacking noises with his lips because of the bread's goodness. "This is without doubt Balthazar's feast," he said. "And is that genuine mutton broth? And sweet corn? I can't believe it . . . it is indeed. I have a surprise for you to go with it. It cost me a pair of shoes, but here it is!" He displayed an oka of wine. "First-class . . . Mavrodaphne!" This surprise he would engulf alone, for the priest withheld alcohol from his family. Before the war it had been different. Nicholos' mother had called it "sunshine in a glass." Her Florentine goblets, too dainty for a Greek home, still stood on a shelf. On cold days in the hill Nicholos had sampled the blood-red shepherd's wine, squirting it from the leather bag deep into the back of his throat. It tasted of turpentine because the bags were tarred, and did not remind him of sunshine.

Nicholos blew on the broth, and little globules of golden fat reflected the lamps like countless moons. He had almost forgotten how meat tasted. During festivals before the war, roasting pits had flared from the dripping of a dozen sizzling sheep. Entrails had cooked with the lamb, thickets of them, wound round and round long spits, and stuffed with nutmeg, garlic, and cloves. The town had reeked of garlic and oil and wine. Saliva came into his mouth as he remembered.

Outside the storm lashed against the thick walls and it felt good to be in dry clothes. He would have been happy were it not for his missing lamb, and silently he asked God to keep it alive for him through the night. If God would do that, he would never distrust God's power again. Then, to put the animal from his mind, he tried to concentrate on the meal and the conversation. Roberto was laughing, and the veins of his temples stood out in the lantern light. "But she was a fine woman," he was saying. "She had more of a mustache than me, but that didn't matter. I liked her. You know I still carry a lock of her hair in the back of my watch. It's always getting the balance wheel clogged up." This was a joke to be laughed at, and Nicholos fabricated a laugh though his thoughts were upon Angela. From the way her lips were tightly closed he suspected that she was worrying about Thanos.

Father Lanaras appeared to listen thoughtfully, his long supple fingers embracing his drinking glass. When he broke in, Nicholos became attentive, for his father seldom reminisced or employed his tongue idly. When he spoke, he addressed the serious present. . . . "The wolves have been destroying flocks up the valley, and they are moving this way. Have you heard the reports?"

"Rumors, yes," said Roberto.

"My friend, you haven't been in this valley when the wolves were starving. Ask my son. Nicholos can tell you how it was in forty-four."

Nicholos would never forget it. With the Germans pulling out and the Andarte taking over, only a few sheep remained, and one bitter-cold night wolves had come down from the mountains. Too late Nicholos had run for the fold, his father close behind him with the gun. The gun had discharged, cutting a bright gash through the tumult of shouts and snapping fangs. The wolves had fled, but in the glow of the lantern Angela held they had discovered the shredded bodies of sheep, throats torn, tongues lolling in lipless mouths. From then on Nicholos and his father had taken turns waiting with the gun. Nicholos had been alone at night when the pack returned, snuffling through the snow. As he had aimed at the moving shadows, a huge body had lunged. Desperately he had swung the muzzle around.

"I remember it well," broke in Roberto. "You don't have to tell me about the winter of forty-four. That prison, with nothing to eat except tortoises! Wolves howled around the camp every night. Skinny as sin, those wolves; if it hadn't been for the wire, we would have been devoured in our sleep. It's queer, the things you remember. The other prisoners began calling me Saint Francis, because I'm from Assisi. They said I should try to tempt the wolves over to the wire. You know how Saint Francis pacified the wolf of Gubbio. Only we would have eaten ours. . . . What a world! A man alone hasn't a chance. Neither does a wolf. We all of us have to hunt in packs."

Nicholos sat with his hands gripping his knees. He gazed into space and saw again the fierce, impersonal eyes, and felt the gun that did not fire. For a second, death had glared at him, and he had somersaulted backward with a great weight pinning him, tearing him. His father had begun shouting and the weight had disappeared. Like some terrible avenging angel, his father had wielded the rifle about his head and brought it down again and again, shouting and cursing and pulverizing the wolf's body until the gunstock broke. Then he had carried Nicholos inside, and though the boy was savagely cut it was not the wounds he remembered clearly, but his father crying, "Why didn't you pull the trigger? Why? Why?"

"I don't know," said Father Lanaras, pushing his plate aside, "I'm not a cruel person. But wolves. . . . I have never regretted killing them."

"They're not the sort of beasts that worry me," said Roberto.

"Not even the white one? There's talk of him."

Nicholos sat up suddenly like a jerked puppet. "The white wolf!"

"That's what they say," admitted Roberto. "The *loup garou!*"

The *loup garou*, born in blasphemy on Christmas Day and doomed to prowl the tombs at night as a wolf. Nicholos had heard the folk tales, had awakened screaming from dreams of that pale hairy man with wounds upon his legs from the bites of dogs. His father had never repeated the werewolf tale, but he had never said there was no such creature, and Nicholos believed in his father's silence. He believed in the wolf that stalked his dreams, with a coat as white as moon-struck silver. No one had ever killed it. The beast was too big for the dogs that tracked it, too big for the men who swung their clubs in the darkness. Only the mountain wastes seemed a match for it, and there, with the war, it had vanished.

"There isn't any such thing as a white wolf," said Angela, who until this moment had been intently regarding the blackened windows.

"But there is. Once in a thunderstorm I saw him!" said Roberto. Here he illustrated the lightning flash by looking heavenward in mock terror from under his raised forearm as though a great light had burst in the sky. "Good God!

41

What a wolf! It was only for a second." The room was silent following this revelation. Angela had turned away from the window. "That was during the war. We were stationed up near the Yugoslavian border, near that dreadful mountain . . . what's its name?"

"You mean Monastir, I think," said Father Lanaras quietly. Only the way his hand absently explored his beard indicated his interest.

"That's it—Monastir. What a devil of a mountain. The peasants there say when great Pan died he was taken to Monastir and buried. Now it's supposed to be haunted by the ghosts of ancient gods, and if you're there long enough, you can't absolutely say the peasants are wrong."

Nicholos felt himself shiver. He was not a coward, but wolves disturbed him more than Andarte, ever since he had faced those devouring eyes. That was how death must be, skulking the mountains, waiting on the hills to come down once or twice a year to Serifos, into the narrow streets, into the dark corners, into the beds of the very old, to take them away. That was a wolf, the white one. That was death.

"Just listen to it out there," said Roberto. He sipped his wine and ran his tongue around his lips. "What a night to be a lonely man." "Or a sheep," thought Nicholos. He heard the big drops falling on the roof, heavy drops splashing on the floor in one corner. Only a fool would choose to go out on such a night, and yet he knew when the opportunity came for him to go unquestioned, he would go and look for Ajax. Otherwise he would not sleep. "This weather makes me realize how much I owe you people, and I feel like a traitor," said Roberto. "But I'm thinking of you. Don't you see why I want them to prepare for the Andarte?"

So it was starting again, that endless, insoluble argument, and Nicholos braced himself to take his father's side.

"Well, that fellow whose sons ran off to the Andarte," said Roberto; "he's been telling everyone at the Modesty that he'll kill both of them with his bare hands. Imagine such hatred. He's drunk and harmless now, but he won't always be. If there's no outlet, not even so much as marching up and down, not even Saint Francis could keep him from murder when the time comes."

Roberto frowned greedily at his wine glass as though annoyed by his thirst. "And it will come, believe me."

"That's true, Father," interjected Angela.

"Let Roberto finish," said Father Lanaras, and Angela got up and strolled across the room; Nicholos watched her head turn sideways as though presenting her ear to the window for some signal from the runaway night.

"All right," said Roberto. "Though we've been through it all. Can you honestly intend to turn the other cheek to an Andarte? Four hundred years ago the Turks took little boys and turned them into Janissaries while you Greeks made up sad songs. It took a bloody war to get rid of the Turks. Four hundred years of preaching and prayer hasn't changed anything. Only now the Andarte are kidnaping girls as well. Either they have to come back as Andarte or remain as hostages against the King's abdication. You can't stop people like that with parables. We have to fight them. There . . . not a word I haven't said before."

"Yes, yes," said Father Lanaras, tapping his finger on the table, "and I have listened time and time again."

"But Roberto's right, Father. How can you deny it?" said Angela, turning from the window. To Nicholos she

43

seemed suddenly and secretly radiant, as though she had received a message.

"There's one thing you don't seem to realize," said Father Lanaras. "Every single town that the Andarte have attacked has in one way or another given provocation. Nothing of the kind has happened here."

"But it will. That Dimitrov. . . ."

"Hold on," said Father Lanaras. "Let me finish. You said yourself the army will be here by morning. That takes matters out of our hands, doesn't it?"

"I don't think so. Within a few days the soldiers will be wandering about hunting shadows. It happened last year. My friend, I'm talking about human nature. If man had arms long enough, he would murder the sun and moon. A saint hasn't a chance, not in this mad world. If he can't protect himself he'll be a slave or a corpse."

"You're wrong," said Father Lanaras. "Men aren't wild animals, and if some behave that way, we must work to change them. Many feel as we do, in their hearts, and together we must strive against that wild beast that would take possession of every one of us."

"And how do you propose to fight this enemy of yours?" asked Roberto.

"Yes, tell us," from Angela.

"By doing the hardest thing in the world. By trying to set an example."

"You mean by doing absolutely nothing," replied Angela, who drummed her fingers on the table in apparent impatience. If Nicholos had been closer, he would have caught hold of those fingers to make her stop, but their father did not seem aware of her sarcasm.

"It must seem that way to some people" was all he said.

44

Roberto shook his head like an old dog bothered by fleas, but Nicholos knew his father was right. Somewhere, sometime, a man must have the courage to break the endless chain of savagery, and if the man were great enough his courage would change the world. Such pacifism had always been his father's way, and during the Hitler war his faith had been tried to the breaking point when the hostages were taken. Father Lanaras had asked to be held in their place, but the German commandant refused to touch a priest. After the hostages were shot, Father Lanaras had confessed to Nicholos how he had sat up in the chapel that night with a rifle in his hands, forcing the bullets into the magazine and finally forcing them out again. Cruelty and hatred had to be paid for, he had told Nicholos, not in like coin, but at a higher price, with love and forgiveness. How terrible *love* and *forgiveness* had sounded, wrenched up from the soul of a man who was almost insane with suffering. As Nicholos knew, love and forgiveness were chains that bound his father's fury, stifled his revenge. That night the man had finally collapsed on his bed, and Nicholos had sat beside him until both had slept. When Nicholos had awakened he had discovered his father's hand were covered with dried blood, from the gouging of his own nails.

"It isn't very comfortable being a sheep when you are hemmed in by wolves," said Roberto.

"It is, if the shepherd is good enough," said Nicholos.

"But is he . . . ever?" asked Angela.

For a split second her quizzical inflection puzzled him. Then she whispered, "Ajax?" and he wanted to hurt back but he was too tired to hurt anyone but himself.

"I'm not pretending it's easy; you have to hold your courage in both hands and pray for it," said Father Lanaras.

"If you are the shepherd, you must look the wolf between the eyes, and make him know that he cannot defeat you even when he has you by the throat."

With jolting suddenness a loud knocking came from the door. Nicholos was nearest, and he turned the knob half expecting a wolf on the threshold. A soldier stood there, his gray-green uniform made darker by the rain. He asked if the priest were home. A convoy of troops had arrived, and he wondered if the chapel might be available for the night.

"For as long as you need it," said Father Lanaras.

It occurred to Nicholos that the harboring of troops was the sort of provocation for which the Andarte were waiting, but he dared not question his father.

"You must be freezing. Can't we get you something hot?" offered Angela.

"I'm all right there, Miss," said the soldier, indicating a bottle protruding from his coat pocket. "Perhaps another time."

"Tomorrow? Would that be all right, Father?"

"Tomorrow we'll be leaving, at first light," said the soldier. Then, brightening, "We'll push them back to Albania this summer."

"There are a great many Andarte up there, I think," said Angela.

"Not enough," said the soldier. "We'll be close to a thousand by morning, with American howitzers."

Did she have to grin that way? Nicholos knew what she was up to, and he stared at her to make her stop.

When the soldier had departed, Father Lanaras had accompanied him to open the chapel and light the lamps. When he returned, he was alone.

46

"Is it wise to have soldiers in the chapel?" asked Nicholos.

"You remember when the Germans were retreating. That was harder," said his father. "But a chapel must shelter everyone."

The Germans had looked very nearly dead, but if he had been his father he would have barred the door. He would have let them freeze to death though his mother was dead forever and he knew revenge could never pay for her loss.

"Bang!" said Roberto. He was sighting at Nicholos over the neck of his empty wine bottle as though it were a rifle. "What about some good cheer? You're a gloomy boy tonight. Your father, too, and Angela mooning at the window. What is this, a conspiracy to make me go home? So we're all doomed! If the Andarte and the wolves don't get us, our neighbors will. Let's see if we can't at least have one last good time." He indicated the desired mood with a moist chuckle. "Now listen! I'm going to propose a toast to your father, and then I want Nicholos to propose. . . ." This way he got them started making up extravagant toasts until all his flesh shook and the others began laughing too. He went to the gramophone and cranked it up. "See?" he said, "see? Now we're having a good time." And they were. Let the world outside drown itself. This was how life should be. "There's only one thing missing," said Roberto. "A dancer. What do you say, Angela?"

As though commanded, Angela went to the center of the room and held her arms arched over her head, her hands limp as lilies. She stood straight, well up on her toes until the music started again. Then she began to glide, the pattern of her dress merging with the motion.

To Nicholos she seemed to move sleepily, like one who

47

holds back energy for a future effort. He felt sure he knew what that effort would be. Later the muffled beam of a flashlight would guide her in the dark.

Roberto cranked the gramophone, then joined Angela in the center of the room. With the music they were off, Angela silently on her toes, Roberto prancing like a clockwork man, lifting heavy shoes in unrestrained mirth. The music drove them round and round the room while Nicholos clapped. It was like the old days when Angela had danced with her father, her feet on his because his steps were long. He did not like the expression on her face as she turned toward him. It wasn't honest, but the same silly grin she had turned on the soldier and on Thanos. When they swung round, Roberto looked funny too. Nicholos stopped clapping. His father had already stopped. The dancers went round once more. Angela's face was averted this time, and there was a faint glow on her cheeks.

Without a word, Father Lanaras rose. Nicholos watched him walk stiffly across the room to remove the needle from the record. The dancers stopped and the room was quiet except for the hissing of the lamps.

"Well, so much for that," said Roberto. He laughed falsely. Everyone was embarrassed. "I congratulate you," he said to Father Lanaras, "on having such a fine dancer in the house. Come, stand beside me and we will drink to the fine dancers of all nations."

"Haven't you had enough wine?" said Father Lanaras. This might have been an overture to a scene, but was not.

"Actually, there doesn't appear to be any more," said Roberto sadly, and Father Lanaras placed his arm around his friend's shoulder as if to say, "I'm sorry for sounding harsh, but after all you've had a good deal of wine and she's my daughter." They sat down again. Roberto's knee joints creaked in the process. "Ah, the pains of getting old," he said. "It's not being old that I really mind; it's feeling young and then having a leg or an arm go back on me."

Angela had moved to the window. She stood again as though looking out, one arm behind her head, shoving back the crown of her dark hair. Nicholos had always thought she was beautiful, but now he saw her good looks as a weapon for her private purposes, and was disturbed.

At last Roberto said softly, "Well, I ought to be going. I've caused enough irritation for one evening."

Father Lanaras also rose, throwing a giant shadow on the white wall. "Look here," he said, "are you sure you can get home alone?"

"Absolutely."

"If you don't mind, please shut the door after you, so it latches."

"Absolutely." Then, with his hand groping for the priest's sleeve, "Did I make a fool of myself?"

"No, you sentimental old idiot. We'll see you tomorrow." Father Lanaras held the door open and Roberto took a step into the rain. Water quickly turned his face into a caricature of dripping tears. It must also have jarred him back into seriousness. "Day after tomorrow," said the Italian, "when you call the meeting, this town will have to make up its mind once and for all."

"With the army here," said Father Lanaras, "I believe it already has."

A flash of lightning illuminated the street; the rain had turned it into a swirling brown stream. Then darkness fell, complete and ominous. Father Lanaras followed the round figure into the storm. "I'll see him home," he called back.

"Listen to the wind," said Angela. "They say a gale like that isn't wind at all, but the angel of death passing over. If it is, his wings must be very wide."

Nicholos felt gooseflesh on his arms, and he thought of Ajax. Would the angel bother with such a small creature?

Evidently sensing Nicholos' discomfort, she added, "Don't worry. I'll help you look tomorrow. We'll find him," and she put her hand lightly on the back of his neck. Nicholos winced.

"What are these frightful marks? Did some animal claw you?"

"Yes, some animal," said Nicholos, shrugging her hand away. "Forget it. There's something I want to know. Are you planning to go out there to meet him?"

"Meet who?"

"You know what I'm talking about," and for emphasis Nicholos closed the great Turkish door, which had been built wide for the passage of oxen. With an effort he locked it and placed the key in his pocket. His father always carried a key.

"What I do is my business," said Angela.

"Not when it has to do with Andarte. They're everybody's business, and you haven't any right. . . ."

"Nicholos, try to understand. . . ."

Her fingers touched his sleeve, lingered there, but Nicholos was in no mood to be reassuring. "And why don't you braid your hair like other girls?" he asked her. The fingers were withdrawn to be clenched at Angela's side.

Angela turned so quickly he could hear the swishing of her skirt. Of course she would do what she pleased. He knew

50

that. The locking of the door was no more than a gesture. He could not keep the future outside, nor could he withhold Angela from a path she seemed bound to take. Nicholos felt certain that before the night was over, both of them would be outside in the storm.

3

Nicholos lay fully clothed under the blankets, fists clenched, staring into the darkness where bright red spots seemed to be swimming. On any other night it would have felt good to be tired and in bed, alone at last. He longed for sleep, but at the last conscious instant, he jolted fully awake, as though a sledge hammer had struck the foot of his bed.

Turning his ear to the beams which slanted down across his bed, Nicholos could hear the murmur of night noises flowing through the weathered wood. Was that Angela stealing away on tiptoe? Did he hear the great key turning, or was it simply the cat hunting mice in the eaves? Did he hear the bleating of sheep? Or was it the call of a night prowler slinking down from the mountains?

Whatever lurked without, he had no choice. With the house finally asleep, he rolled to the edge of the bed. No light showed from Angela's room. Unless she had already gone, she would be asleep. His feet touched the floor.

The only exit took him through Angela's room, and the beating of his heart seemed loud enough in his own ears to wake the dead. When his groping foot found the trap door, it was open, and he almost fell through. Accompanied by the sad creaking of his leather belt, he started down. Three tiptoed steps brought him to the door. With his hand on the knob he took one last deep breath and stepped out into the night.

The gale tore at his hair and a thin drizzle crept inside his collar. With his hand on the wall he moved up the cobbled street; the shallow stream beds had filled and the water was descending from level to level.

As he passed the fold, Nicholos heard the bells of the flock. He knew it was the last friendly sound he would hear unless good luck brought to his ears the voice of his lost lamb. He expected no other living creature to be abroad. The Andarte, the wolves would all have found shelter, but as he climbed he was not alone. With him were the stories of childhood: shapeless horrors stooping in shadows, vampires sprung from the spider-woven earth, and phantom dancers to lure the lonely shepherd.

Nicholos rested frequently. His feet were so heavy with mud that he seemed to be moving the entire earth at every step. When he paused, he listened for the sound of a bell, and looked about in the occasional shudderings of lightning. The silhouette of the old German tank seemed at first to have animal form, to move. He took a step backward, and then the lightning came. Not even the white wolf could be that large.

Under the shelter of the cemetery's upper wall, he paused. Angela was right. He was a fool, and when he heard faint laughter he was sure his imagination was getting out of hand. A yellow flap of light from the turret of the old tank was real enough, but before it seemed to hover a grotesque gorilla shape which, as he watched, divided into two smaller forms. One of these settled back inside the turret, while the other leaped down and rapidly disappeared toward Serifos.

Nicholos scaled the wall. He did not look back for fear of seeing something following him, but in his imagination a hand was extended behind him, long and pale and covered with scars left by dogs. It reached for his shoulder. Nicholos ran, slipped, and landed on his knees in the mud. After that he forced himself to walk and listen, until he reached the spot around which the shepherds of Serifos were accustomed to swing wide on their journeys to and from the village. They called it the place of the tall stones, because of the circle of great boulders raised on end. Nicholos had heard from his father that it was an ancient shrine dedicated to Lycaean Zeus, but for him it was the place of execution; the place where the hostages had been shot. He would have followed the roundabout path had he not seen a glow of light on the boulders. In the partial shelter of the rocks a struggling fire bathed the surrounding stones in oily orange light. Squatting around the blaze were human shapes, their long hair bound back with black ribbons. Andarte! He counted eight of them, eating silently, ravenously, tearing with bare hands and knives at something that turned above the flames. Its pale nostrils wide, its black mouth bubbling, the skinned body of a lamb was spitted over the fire. Nicholos saw it all with unbearable outrage. Almost raw, Ajax was being devoured! He wanted to topple the boulders upon them, to scream until their ears burst; but they carried automatic weapons and he had only his fury. Heedless of stones and trees, he ran wildly from the place.

In that reckless flight he thought only of putting an end

54

to the feast. When he came to his own street he did not hesitate, but ran until he leaned, panting, against the chapel door. Inside, he blundered over the forms of sleeping soldiers toward a candle burning in a corner. There four soldiers played at backgammon with bits of painted bone.

"Here, what's all this!" said one, whose nose had a twist toward the end which gave him the appearance of smelling sideways at something unpleasant.

Standing before them, Nicholos was momentarily silenced by the flesh-and-blood reality of the men.

"He's all right. He's the priest's boy," said another. "Tell us, lad; what's all the excitement?" and in an incoherent rush Nicholos told what he had seen.

"You think they'll still be there?" asked the captain. He was clearly reluctant to leave the chapel, but in the end he called a platoon together.

"What will you do to them?" asked Nicholos. He was worried now, for the men were checking their weapons.

"If it's just as you say," said the captain, "there won't be any need for shooting," but he was pushing cartridges into the cylinder of a revolver, and the sound of the hammer clicking back was like the snapping of knuckle bones.

Thirty soldiers, rifles loaded and at the ready, followed Nicholos from the chapel. He led with growing reluctance. Fatigue and apprehension had begun to outweigh his fury, but it was too late, and he went up the muddy slope with a sense of unreality. He found himself wishing that the glow would not be on the boulders, but it was still there, and the soldiers crept forward in a widening circle until the shrine was surrounded.

Nicholos prayed that the Andarte would surrender. They had no chance. A command barked out and for a pro longed moment all action was suspended. The soldiers crouched with rifles aimed, the Andarte with food bulging their cheeks. In that instant Nicholos' heart no longer beat. Then one of the Andarte stood up. He whirled to face the voice with a cup of coffee in his hands. In the dark, a soldier must have made a mistake. One shot and then many rattled within the stone walls like firecrackers set off in a barrel. Before Nicholos' horrified eyes the Andarte seemed to dive for holes in the solid ground while bullets struck sparks off the stones. One figure ran toward him, waving his arms, shrieking, "I want to surrender! I want to surrender!" Nicholos recognized him as Stavro Dimitrov.

Conscious only of the other's peril, Nicholos shoved through the ring of boulders into a darkness full of bright stabbings. Wildly he grappled with Stavro and bore him down. How many times could they kill seven men? "Stop it! Stop it!" Nicholos screamed with his lips against a stone and the taste of blood in his mouth. Then a blunt fist struck the back of his head. He had no thoughts any more. Sleep carried him down.

"Nicholos, are you asleep?" It was Angela's voice, vibrant as though she were casting a spell.

He was in his own bed.

"You gave Father a scare. What an idiot you are!" He could tell she was relieved. "Look here; I've found an egg for you." With this rarity came other breakfast delicacies: feta cheese, honey, and strong sweet coffee.

"Where's Father?" he asked, confused.

"Up there still, I guess. One of them wanted a priest. It's queer, when they say God doesn't exist, to suddenly want a priest, just because they're dying."

For Nicholos, the room darkened perceptibly. "Then it wasn't a dream," he said. For the sin he had committed, it seemed appropriate that God should strike him dead. He closed his eyes so tightly there were bright whirlings behind his lids.

"What's wrong, Nicholos? Does your head still hurt?"

"I hurt all over . . . Angela, do you know what happened last night?"

"Yes."

"And you don't mind?"

"Why should I? I didn't know any of them except Stavro. He thinks you're quite a hero."

"Is he all right?"

"Not a scratch. Father has him. It took some talking to keep him from the army. You'd have been proud of Father."

"Do you know what I did, last night?" insisted Nicholos.

"Of course I do, you big idiot. After I warned you over and over again, still you had to risk getting killed for a lamb. I don't understand you." Her inflection implied that she did understand, but found him exasperatingly stupid.

"I don't mean about Ajax." Haltingly, he explained how he had informed on the Andarte.

"I see," she said, her voice noncommittal.

He wanted to be held tight and forgiven, but he knew he was too old for that to help.

"You will feel better if you eat, Nicholos."

Angela held the coffee to his lips, but it was sickeningly sweet and his throat rebelled at the sediment in the bottom of the cup.

"I must have been crazy," he said.

"Perhaps, for a little while."

"Father will despise me."

"I doubt that. He never hates anyone. And besides, he doesn't know the whole story. I thought you just happened to be there, looking for the lamb. Why should he think otherwise? When the soldiers came to the house, they said you'd fallen on Stavro and gotten hurt with a chip of rock. There isn't any reason for Father to know any more."

"But *I* know. I always will."

"Stop feeling sorry for yourself. It wasn't your fault. You did what anyone would have done. You were a hero last night, or Stavro wouldn't be alive now. Look at it that way."

Nicholos nodded and grinned at his sister a grin no deeper than the skin that tightened over his cheekbones. "You aren't going to tell Father?" he asked.

"I wasn't planning to . . . that's funny though. Now you're keeping secrets from poor Father. He tries so hard for the world to be perfect no one wants to tell him it isn't."

"I want to confess to him myself, that's all."

"Why? To make him miserable? That's all the good it will do, you know. . . . Nicholos, what does it take to wake you up? If you can't bear the thought of messing up your clean little soul, you'd better retire to a monastery." Angela got up and walked to the window. "I'm sorry . . . that was nasty. It's almost morning; I can just make out the mountains. Someone will have to take the flock out."

She might treat it as just another day, but he could not. He had failed himself and his father. He had caused the death of seven human beings, and if God refused to punish him directly he must go to his father for judgment. Until then he would try not to think about it.

"Angela, you were out last night, weren't you?"

"Why do you say that?"

"Your shoes . . . they're muddy, so I thought . . ."

"I was, for a while."

"Were you at the tank, seeing him? Thanos?"

He expected to be put off, but was not. She even contrived a laugh. "So that was you in the graveyard. What a fright! I've never run so fast in my life."

"But why always Thanos?"

"You know why, Nicholos. . . . We aren't going to quarrel, are we?" With the flat of her palm she stroked the top of his hair gently, as she would stroke the head of a dog. "Have I changed so much?" She wanted him to say no, and he did because he wanted to please her.

"Oh, yes," she quietly contradicted. "I have. We all have."

Outside it was still dark, but there was the smell and the feel of dawn which comes before the light.

When they were younger, they had understood one another completely. They had grown up together as naturally as puppies, but lately, since the partition had been erected between their sleeping compartments, Angela had become aloof. It was as though she had fallen heir to some totally feminine secret. Ever since his victory on the wall, it seemed she had been moving into a future where he could not follow. He wanted to explain this to her, to show that he understood and that he wasn't blaming her. He was afraid for her, that was all.

Nicholos spoke very slowly, as though groping through dark. "You won't be going away, or anything, will you?"

"What in the world do you mean by that?"

"I just thought. . . ." She was staring at him out of her wonderful dark eyes, as though from a high terrace of her own growing. Her smile was beautiful. As always, it moved Nicholos to forgive everything. "What I thought was . . .

well, the way you talk, you must hate it here, Angela. Isn't that right?" She looked at him sadly, then dropped her eyes. "You mean I'm right?"

"Don't I usually seem happy?" she asked.

"I guess so, but the way you're always talking about other places, and going off at night to see Thanos. . . ." Nicholos dreaded a day that seemed inevitable, when she too would forsake him.

"Oh, Nicholos . . . sometimes when I listen to you, it's as though I were talking to myself. What if I said I was two persons, and one of them would give anything to get away, to do things; but the other person is afraid. She's a little girl and she doesn't want to grow up. She wants to go on loving her father and brother very much. It's the other one who makes fun of Father, and lectures you sometimes."

"I know that, Angela."

"Don't you think I know the world would be a better place if everyone were like you and Father? But I think you love me enough to help me be bad, if you knew that was what I wanted."

"Listen, Angela. . . ."

"Sleep, Nicholos. Stop worrying about me and don't think too much. It doesn't agree with you."

Without warning, the shutters clattered. Window glass shivered in the frames and explosions followed.

Angela leaped from her chair as though physically propelled by the concussion. At the window, she threw back the shutters and the red sun burst inside. Nicholos shielded his eyes.

"What's going on?"

"Artillery," she told him.

He joined her at the window. There was haze still on

the peaks and a battery of four howitzers was firing into the mist: the spring offensive against the Andarte had begun. The howitzers were soon joined by other batteries, then by infantry, all firing into the retreating mist. The soldiers from the chapel formed ranks in the streets. Nicholos could hear the barking of commands followed by the tramp of feet. Above the cemetery the men were spreading out into a skirmish line. An immensity of rock loomed before them as they moved forward, antlike from this distance, to attack.

Angela breathed deeply of the morning air. "Strange, it's really a lovely spring morning," she said. But for Nicholos, even nature's bright promise seemed stolen from the world. Only cruelty and death remained, and they were his enemies.

4

Nicholos watched the heavy flight of the owls, driven from the Judas tree by the sudden clamor of the bell. It sounded first near, then far, resounding from the blue bowl of sky above Serifos. Everyone must hear it; even the soldiers camped in the hills. Only the eagles seemed not to notice. Nicholos envied the great birds their immunity.

The ringing stopped. His father emerged from the arched doorway of the chapel. Roberto accompanied him, and Nicholos heard the pair debating. Roberto still wanted to arm the town. But this was his father's domain, and he had called his congregation together to talk about wolves and the disposition of their prisoner. The meeting would prove who was stronger. Now Father Lanaras placed his hand for a moment on Roberto's shoulder. Slowly it dropped, and Father Lanaras walked inside the chapel. Sad as his father seemed, Nicholos had no doubt he would win the congregation, and the talk of fighting would end. It had to. Nicholos was more than ever persuaded of his father's views because of their talk the day before. Hesitantly, he had approached his father to confess, and when he had done so his father had said, "Come here; sit by me."

"I can't," he had said. "I told you, I killed them."

"I heard from the soldiers that you led them, Nicholos."

"Can't you punish me, then?" he had asked. But what physical punishment could equal the gravity of his offense?

"Sit down, Nicholos. I will tell you something."

Nicholos could not bear the look in his father's eyes. He had sat down with his gaze on the floor.

"Punishing you won't make it right before God," his father had said.

"With you?"

"Not with me, either. Nothing is ever forgotten, Nicholos."

"But what will you do?"

"I'll do nothing. It's not up to me, but you must live with it, Nicholos."

"For the rest of my life?"

"A man must be responsible for his actions."

The burden of his sins had seemed intolerable, and he would have cried if crying had not seemed an easy escape. His father must have expected him to cry, for he put his arms around Nicholos and pressed his son's face close against the stiff black wool of his robe. "Perhaps you will learn a lesson from this," he had said. "It's never a person's intention to do evil, but he does evil because he lacks the strength to do good. Another time, you will control your anger, Nicholos. You will remember what a terrible thing it is to see young men die. . . . There is something I have never told you. As a young man, when I lived in Smyrna, we Greeks wanted to take Asia Minor away from Turkey. We fought, and I led the village men. We were beaten, and the Turks followed us to our village. The priest was the only man who did not hide. I can still see the purple umbrella he carried in the summer. When they couldn't find us, they barricaded him inside the chapel and burned it to the ground. It was as though I had killed him with my own hands. Perhaps that is why I am a priest today, and why I did nothing when your mother died. It is a dreadful thing to take a human life. A man is not the same afterward. I do not even like to go before the congregation and urge them to kill the wolves. You know, the gypsies say man and the animals are a brotherhood, and though I'm not capable of it myself, there have been men who have made friends with wolves. Those are the saints."

Twenty-four hours had passed since their talk. It had stayed with Nicholos ever since, and with it came a lifting of his spirits and a resurgence of love for his father.

Now at the chapel door, Father Lanaras again put his arm around Nicholos. "Look after Stavro," he said. "Tell him nothing will happen to him." Nicholos took the heavy key from his father and went to the small chamber behind the chapel where Stavro had been imprisoned. He unlocked the door and entered. Stavro, who had been fumbling with his leather snake boots, stood up sharply and turned around.

"You'll be needing new ones," said Nicholos. Stavro looked confused, his hands clasped awkwardly across his stomach. "Shoes, I mean. You really tore that one."

"Oh yes . . . on the stones," answered Stavro, still distracted, continuing to stand with arms locked around his body as though he were cold.

To Nicholos it seemed strange that this boy, younger than he by half a year and more naturally tenderhearted, should have run away with his brother. He had none of

64

Thanos' ferocity. Bathed and clad in Nicholos' clothes, he looked more like a smooth-cheeked choirboy than an Andarte fighter. That was the impression Father Lanaras wished him to make upon the congregation should he be called before them.

"Don't worry. Father won't let anything bad happen to you. He asked me to tell you that," said Nicholos, but he was not as confident as he sounded. He remembered his father's conversation with Stavro. "Whatever crimes you have committed that my congregation may know about," his father had said, "tell them to me now, so that I will not be taken unaware when I stand before them in the house of God." Stavro had confessed immediately. His one mission, the assassination of Roberto Bellofatto, had failed when he saw children playing on the teacher's doorstep. Instead of throwing the bomb at the house, he had thrown it away into the cemetery. "And nothing more?" Father Lanaras had asked. "They know about the bomb. Have you planted mines on the road? Shot anyone? Burned any homes?" Stavro had denied all except the bomb, and for that and his association with the Andarte he was in peril of his life. An insufficient crime, it seemed to Nicholos, yet he knew his friend was terrified by the way he stood crouched over, from the giddy pitch of his voice.

"Has anyone come yet?" asked Stavro. "Have you seen my father?"

"No one yet." Nicholos remembered what Roberto had said of Dimitrov.

"Would it be all right if we went to the chapel . . . for a moment?"

Before his disappearance, Stavro had visited the chapel regularly, and Nicholos now swung open the door. Inside, the

65

air was balmy with incense. The chapel itself was highly worked in Byzantine artistry so that entering it was like going into a paradise full of towering flowers and monstrous birds and beasts. Adam and Eve wandered on the painted walls, while above them, like colossal butterflies, angels were flying. Nicholos lit a candle before the altar, which was heaped with dried garlands of jasmine and wreaths of camomile and pinks. He crossed himself from left to right, then stooped to the smoke-blackened icon, whose surface left a brassy consolation on his lips.

Stavro hugged the altar rail, making votive offerings tinkle with his anxiety. He seemed to want more, a smile from the fixed lips. Nicholos turned away, pretending to examine the walls to give some privacy to his friend's appeal. "Will all be well, dear sweet disciple of Christ?" Nicholos traced with his finger along a bulge in the plaster where an ancient column showed. Then he heard voices outside, and he roused Stavro. "Don't let it happen, don't make me have to . . ." the boy was saying, but Nicholos took his arm and led him back to the private cell, behind the iconostasis. Closing the heavy door, he said, "It's like a fortress here," and, because Stavro had always seemed deeply devout, "a fortress of God," he added softly. No place in Serifos was really safe for an Andarte, he knew. Only the mountains were. Through the narrow window high in the wall he could see them, and the slowly turning eagles.

"It's all right," Stavro said at last. "Everything will be all right," as though it were Nicholos who needed encouragement. "You've done everything you could. You saved my life." It was true. A human life had fallen into his hands and he had preserved it. Nicholos felt a surge of responsibility.

"What's going on, Stavro? What are you hiding under your shirt?" Nicholos asked.

Stavro shook his head, too vehemently it seemed. "I'm just cold," he said.

Villagers were arriving. With the door ajar, Nicholos could see his father sprinkling some with holy water, touching their foreheads with basil as they advanced to kiss the cross and his hand. These were the faithful who believed in God and in Father Lanaras. They all seemed to him warm and nervous and bound together by countless old friendships. Nicholos felt sure they would discuss only the wolves.

Those who had fought with Zervas in the war, Dimitrov who led them in bitter talk, were not present. Few of the shepherds had come, either, only old Mavrudes, kilted, shaggy-haired, gentle of voice, with those who followed him.

So far as Nicholos was concerned, it was for the best. Even Dimitrov's absence was a good thing, though he could hardly explain to Stavro, who kept asking if his father was in the crowd. "You'd think he'd come. He's very strong against the Andarte, I suppose, but we got on. It was only Thanos who fought with him."

"He'll probably come along later," said Nicholos. He wanted to be firm and collected, an example of calm for his friend, but the room seemed terribly close. "Probably you won't have to go to a camp. You can stay with us. Maybe help with the sheep when things settle down. Remember the fun we used to have? Going barefoot in the grass, and lying on our backs in it with nothing to do but watch the sheep all day."

"I remember how we'd dig a little trench and make the big black crickets race."

"We'll do that, too," said Nicholos, and he would have

given anything to be out of this tiny whitewashed prison, up on the hill. He would lie so still in the tall grass that a butterfly would land on his nose and he would feel the slow beat of its powdery wings. That was far from here, that was peace.

"Listen, what are you trying to hide from me?" Nicholos asked.

"Nothing."

"Under your shirt; I know you've got something there."

Stavro appeared silently intent upon the crowd in the chapel. At first glance he seemed calm, indifferent to Nicholos' inquiry. Then Nicholos caught sight of the rise and fall of the boy's chest. Just left of center, his heartbeat was visible.

Nicholos was about to insist when he heard the first confident words of his father's speech. Nicholos thrilled to his father's church voice. It was no ordinary voice, but a voice half God's. "First we must speak of a boy . . . Stavro Dimitrov. You all know him. He used to play with your children . . . and mine. Now he is called an Andarte, if a boy so young can be anything but a boy. Most of you know that he threw a bomb."

"They're all spellbound; you should see them," said Nicholos, glancing at his friend. "Hey, what's that?" Stavro held something shiny which he tried to hide. Nicholos made a grab for it, and just as suddenly drew back, horrified. In his hands, Stavro held a tiny pistol. "You're crazy! Where did. . . ? If they knew you had that thing . . . give it to me!" But Stavro held the gun like a drowning man clutching a life preserver.

"Give it to me, Stavro."

Stavro raised the gun, aimed it. His face was dreadfully controlled. "Don't!" he said. "Don't come any closer. . . .

68

Please, Nicholos, sit down. Tell me what they're saying."
Nicholos sat with his back to Stavro, his ear to the door.
"You're my best friend, but don't you see, they want to kill
me! Nicholos . . . you can see that. . . . What else can
I do?"

Nicholos understood his friend's fears, but a gun was
madness. To fight his way out would be suicide. Others
might die too, and this Nicholos had to prevent. He tried
to explain to Stavro, but all the other said was, "Tell me,
what are they saying?"

"The schoolmaster is talking," said Nicholos. "Now he's
telling how you were supposed to throw the bomb at him,
but how you decided to kill the dead instead. Listen, there's
nothing to fear. Can't you hear them laughing?" Outside,
whatever malice toward Stavro the crowd might have had was
dissolved in mirth. "Do you hear them, Stavro?" Nicholos
stood up slowly, and turned. The gun trembled, and Stavro
stared at him as though his future depended on the unswerv-
ing steadiness of his gaze. It was a cry for help, a surrender.
The pistol sank down and Nicholos took it gently away. "You
wouldn't have used it anyway," he said.

"It was Thanos. He got me to sew it into the top of my
boot." Stavro sounded as though he were about to cry from
sheer relief.

Outside, Roberto had advocated the priest's custody of
the boy. No one protested, and the meeting moved on. Father Lanaras was saying, "There has been talk of using poison
to destroy the wolves, but I cannot condone this method, and
I will tell you why. First, there are innocent animals. . . ."
Nicholos decided he need fear no more for Stavro, but there
still remained the question of arming Serifos. He saw Ro-

berto rise to his feet and lean his fingers on the back of the chair before him.

"We have agreed with Father Lanaras regarding the boy. I believe we are all in agreement with what he has to say about wolves, but there is something else. The survival of Greece is being threatened while we talk of sheep. Listen . . . here are the facts." He held up a sheet of paper and brandished it. "In Kotta there were two hundred children. Forty are left. In Nimfaion, one hundred fifty-three; now there are six. Six! In Serifos we have not so many to spare. When the Andarte come to burn and steal our children, will you turn the other cheek? That is what Father Lanaras would have us do. Only an angel can do that; an angel, or a lamb. You will say the soldiers have come to destroy the Andarte. Didn't they promise the same thing last year? Perhaps Father Lanaras will argue that we must consider our immortal souls, but no vision of hell can compare with the realities we now face. These Andarte pillage and kill, not as soldiers, but as wild beasts. They are the wolves we should be preparing for. . . ."

"Listen to him. Listen to him shout!" whispered Stavro. "He'll have them in here after me. The door won't stop them."

"No, that won't happen. He wouldn't have joked before," said Nicholos, but he couldn't help studying the long brass bolts and three brass hinges, wondering how long they could hold.

"If they start hammering on the door, I'll let you escape. You could make it through the window," said Nicholos.

"No, it's too high. I couldn't."

"I'll help you. The mountains aren't far."

"I'm not going to try," said Stavro. "Just listen at the door. Tell me what's happening!"

As quietly as possible Nicholos closed and locked the great door, but he could still hear the debate, and through the door's large keyhole he could make out his father. He heard his father laugh.

"When he laughs like that, he's angry," Nicholos said. "I think he's going to take care of the schoolteacher."

Father Lanaras' voice came to them through the door with the patient force of a cresting tide. "Roberto, as all of you know, is my very close friend. He is a very good schoolteacher as well, and he was a good soldier in his day. But Serifos is a quiet town, and except for a few broken tombstones and paint scrawled on the walls, the Andarte have left it alone. Two days ago the army was here. They are in the mountains now, dealing with the Andarte.

"In Jesus' name, no more talk of turning Serifos into a fortress! It is devil's madness. The wolves are real and deadly. They are natural enemies which God gives us strength to combat. We will fight the wolves, then, not other men. If you do not think my reasons for calling you together are sufficient, let me tell you the news from Grevena. An entire flock has been ravaged by wolves . . . an entire flock! And the shepherd who was there swears he saw among them the white wolf of Monastir!"

The congregation stirred. His father held them now with a terror that had haunted their childhood, and Nicholos thought of the tracks he had seen on the hillsides. He had heard wolves at night these last weeks, moaning in their hunger. "I am a man of my word," said Father Lanaras. "We have had to combat wolves before. You all remember the last time. If we had not fought them, there would be no

71

sheep, no poultry, nothing but a little bread, maybe an olive, to eat in this valley." His words reverberated, echoing across the ceiling where rounded panels sent back a medley of sounds as though the painted angels were disputing.

Nicholos had no doubt about his father's victory. The congregation was excited about the wolves, while Roberto slouched in his chair, beaten. All that remained was a final vote on the measures to be taken, when there came the sound of feet approaching. Nicholos had never heard anyone run so fast. They turned the corner of the chapel, clipped like a rain of nails across the stone terrace. The door burst open and an unfamiliar voice shouted, "Hurry! The Andarte have set fire to the orchards!"

The chapel emptied quickly. Nicholos was torn between his desire to follow the excitement and his duty to the prisoner. He looked at Stavro, jerked his arms against his sides. This was desertion, but he had to go.

"I'm afraid," Stavro whispered hopelessly; "I'm terribly afraid . . . will you leave the gun?"

"Listen, there's nothing to fear," said Nicholos. "You heard them . . . and with this great door locked, nothing can bother you. I have the key around my neck, see? It's a fortress, remember?" and he went out, and turned the heavy key. He had to ride on it with his entire weight to make it work.

Nicholos pursued the crowd which hurried off with an awful air of calamity. He heard the footsteps ahead, muffled by patches of mud and then resounding on the whitewashed stones along the alleys. It was a hard run, with the gun in his pocket galling his leg, and he did not catch up with the leaders until he met them returning. All a false alarm. There was no fire. The green orchard lay under an evening sky from which all color was emptying. Not even the distant pine forests, which the Andarte had fired weeks before, were smoking.

Nicholos walked back to the chapel with his father, who said, "It went well today. I was worried for some time. If it hadn't been for the soldiers . . . well, God willing, Serifos will survive this war." He seemed happy, his walk was jaunty. "With the boy on our hands, we'll have to stretch the food somehow. There's Christo, too . . . he hasn't been around lately. I hope his feet aren't troubling him."

"No," said Nicholos, "he was up in the meadow a few days ago. His feet were fine."

They turned the corner and approached the chapel. It was deserted, silent. "Stavro will be your responsibility as well as mine," said Father Lanaras. "We can't have him slipping off."

"I don't believe he would want to go back," said Nicholos. He was happy for the first time since Ajax had disappeared. From all the horror at least one friendship had been salvaged, and it surprised him how important that seemed.

They entered the chapel. Nicholos saw at once that the great door to the private cell hung ajar, splintered by axes. "Andarte!" He had no doubt that they had taken Stavro, but Father Lanaras flung the huge door aside and rushed to the bench where the boy had sat. "God! Don't let it be!" he cried. In his hand he held a rusty razor. "It's not Andarte. It's Dimitrov!"

Nicholos' thoughts whirled like mice in a wheel. A terrible dread seemed to suck the air from his lungs. There wasn't enough air left in the chapel for him to catch his breath, and he rushed outside. He called his friend by name, as though Stavro might be playing at hide and seek. He listened, called again.

From across the darkening hillside, through the thick gray air of evening there came five shots, then silence.

Nicholos sat down. He would have fallen otherwise. Dumbly, without thoughts, without sensation, he watched his father rush away. He saw the crowd return, full of questions. Angela came to him. She told him that Stavro was dead, shot down in the place of the stones.

"Come home, Nicholos. It's not the end of the world." She pulled at his hand, but he would not go with her.

Now his father was returning and the throng made way for him. He held something in his arms that looked little, and flat, and Nicholos could see that some of them were afraid to look, while others stood on tiptoe, gaping.

"This is the body of a boy. Look at him!" shouted Father Lanaras, his face streaming tears. "Whoever killed him has invited death into our village. His murderers must confess, or this boy will lie under a field of new corpses. There will be no end to vengeance . . . for the love of God!" Here the voice broke and Father Lanaras hurried on with his burden, passing Nicholos, forcing his way through the crowd toward the chapel door. The mob followed. Dazed and uncaring, Nicholos felt himself being trampled. Someone tripped over his leg, turned and cursed him. Christo was with the others, and his face bore the same expression of enthralled curiosity. Nicholas tried to rise and follow his father, but managed only to support himself against the chapel wall. There, trembling like an overtaxed engine, he was horribly sick.

A voice began shouting in the street. "Do you think

the Andarte will spare us? There's no choice now." It was Roberto. Fists were brandished and many voices were raised. Nicholos witnessed it all without feeling, still leaning against the rough cool wall of the chapel. Too much had been demanded of his emotions. They were numb. He knew only one thing: behind the faces of all men were the faces of beasts. He knew that now.

He groped his way to the chapel door. His father knelt before the iconostasis, his forehead resting against it in the patient suffering attitude of an ox. Stavro lay beside him, his face uncovered and cocked slightly forward as though to study the punctures in his own chest. Blood still flowed from the wounds in a hemorrhage that spread slowly, blackening the ancient mosaics. From the marble face, already fixed in death, the eyes transmitted through half-closed lids all the secrets of life and death. For a moment, Nicholos stood there and he could look at the face. It wasn't Stavro's at all. Stavro was in the hills, forever. It was death lying there, death quietly promising to fill up the world with blood.

Outside in the street people were carrying bundles. Dumbly he watched their excitement as they built up a barricade at the end of the alley. They were noisy; they looked happy, like children playing with blocks. But Nicholos was conscious only of death flowing out from the chapel. It would drown them all.

5

A breeze swept up the honey-colored slopes to the hilltop meadow where Nicholos kept his flock. It was good to be far from Serifos, which five rifle shots had turned into an alien town. The shopkeepers now kept weapons behind their counters, and the bulge of a pistol below the belt had become an accepted feature of masculine apparel.

From his hillside it still looked the same. The other shepherds and the farmers were up with the sun. The Modesty Café had opened its doors and a tentative table appeared each morning under the mulberry tree. Refugees still moved along the road, though he saw fewer of them now. His father went regularly to the chapel and called on his parishioners as he had always done, but there were changes in his father, too. Something had gone out of him, and he pursued his tasks not as a leader of the village but as one who performs an endless and useless chore.

When Nicholos had expressed his concern to Angela, she had replied, "You know, the trouble with Father is that what happens to other people happens to him. There's a book

76

about a knight called Don Quixote. Have you heard of him?" Nicholos had not. "Well, anyway, Father's like him, I think. This knight tries so hard all the time, but the world isn't what he thinks it is, so nothing works out. He messes up everything . . . now don't look angry every time I criticize Father." Actually, Nicholos had not been angry, but the truth of what she had said made him sad. It seemed true about himself as well. It even seemed to explain why Stavro was dead.

Nicholos lacked the capacity for endless speculation. Legs crossed, he sat glumly beside a mountain pool and examined his reflection. He was not fond of that narrow, rather brooding face with the high cheekbones. Without smiling, he stuck out his tongue, and as he did so another image trembled beside his own on the dark mirror of the pool. Nicholos turned as he recognized the intruder, and the stern lines of his weathered young face relaxed in an answering smile.

Christo had arrived stealthily. From under a thatch of unruly hair, he fixed Nicholos with crafty eyes. Then he smiled suddenly, and ran.

"Bang, bang! You're dead!" shouted Nicholos.

Christo fell on the grass, and when Nicholos walked over to him, he said, "Let's play wounded. You can bandage me."

"Where are you hit, Sergeant?"

"In the arm, Captain. But I'm not going to cry."

"You're a brave soldier. Tell me how it happened."

"Ambush. Ten bullets. Machine gun." Christo indicated a fatal pattern of hits across his chest.

"But you went on fighting?"

"Yes, Captain, I killed every one of the enemy and I raised the flag."

"You deserve a medal, Sergeant. Here it is," and he tickled Christo until the child giggled loudly, helplessly. "You're getting to be a fat one, you know that?"

"Nicholos, suppose the Andarte really come. Would they kill us?"

"They won't come," he said. There had been no trace of the Andarte for several weeks, and Serifos was ready for them now.

"But what's it like, being killed?" asked Christo.

"Horrible."

"I mean, what's it really like?"

"How should I know?" Death was a great mystery. Nicholos could not imagine his own dying. Deep down he felt sure he was never going to die. He, Nicholos Lanaras, was unique. Death was for others, and in this respect God had made him differently, had designed him for some superhuman purpose.

"Are you afraid to think about dying?" asked Nicholos. When Christo said that he was, Nicholos told him the story of the man who went to a land where death was never mentioned and where there were no graveyards. "We know nothing of death," they said. "When a man's time comes, an angel appears on the hillside and calls his name." Years later, when the man was at the barber shop being shaved, the angel appeared and called his name, and the man ran to greet the angel without waiting for the other side of his face to be shaved.

"The Andarte aren't like that," said Christo. "They'd take us away whether we want to go or not."

"Not if we're careful and look out for ourselves," said Nicholos. That was the philosophy he had learned from Angela. "When everything else is burning down, there is

78

only one thing that matters," she had told him. "Me! Me! Me! . . . Understand?" and they had chosen a hiding place in case Serifos was attacked. Nicholos wanted to tell Christo about it, but that was not part of the "me" philosophy and he refrained.

"But they come at night, without any warning."

"I know, but don't worry. I'll look after you," said Nicholos. Already he was having difficulty with the new philosophy. "Besides, the army's taking care of things." This wasn't true. Only the other day survivors from Votokhorion had arrived, and Christo told him so. "They had to sign sugar-ration cards, but they didn't know how to read, most of them, and they were really signing requests for their children to be taken."

"Hey, listen," said Nicholos, "have you ever heard of cricket racing? It's great fun . . . this is what you've got to do. . . ."

They played at cricket racing as he had done long ago with Stavro until the first red trace of evening entered the sky. Then they started for home.

"What's that over there?" asked Christo. In the east there was a growing brilliance, as though the sun were rising and setting at the same time. "It looks like a giant trying to set fire to the sky."

Nicholos realized the pine forests were burning. The distant flames stood motionless along the mountain ridges. When they reached the cemetery with the flock, a few villagers had come up to watch. They carried guns, and one of them said the fires had been set by the Andarte to keep the soldiers busy. Nicholos could not understand how the burning forests would bother the soldiers. Only the foresters would really mind, and they were men without politics.

"Where are you going?" he asked the men.

"After wolves," said Dimitrov the butcher.

"Tonight?"

"Give me a pitch-dark night when the wolves aren't shadow-shy," said the butcher.

Others were arriving, and all were armed. While Nicholos waited they started off. Dimitrov led them toward the forest path. For a moment they were silhouetted against the brightening flames and then they were gone. He wondered why he had not heard about the hunt, and whether his father knew. It bothered him that the others followed Dimitrov, a man who apparently had killed his own son.

"Come on," he said to Christo; "it's getting dark." They prodded the sheep along to the barricade of wine barrels above the chapel. There Nicholos helped the sentinel, a boy not much older than himself, to roll one of the barrels aside.

"Hey, Stratos, are you the only one left to guard the town?"

"Listen, when I fight I'm a demon," replied Stratos.

They rolled the creaking barrel back into place.

"Stay well, Stratos," he said.

"*Yasas*," called the sentry.

It was dark now. The distant fire brightened the fading day. Why had the Andarte set it? Surely not to harass the foresters or the army. He was not certain, but wasn't it possible that Dimitrov was leading the men into a trap?

Nicholos counted the sheep as they entered the fold, locked the gate, and turned toward home. Summer vapors still rose hot from the sun-baked sidewalks. He knew the house would be too hot for sleep, but that was all right since he had no intention of going to bed.

Lanterns flickered as the villagers hurried home for fear

of the Andarte. Far off, sad as sunset on the last day of summer, came a faint far call. A wolf was howling at the new moon. "Listen," said Nicholos. "Do you hear him?" He took Christo by the hand.

In front of the house they met Angela. Barefoot, she was scouring the doorstep. When she noticed them she stood up, straightened her skirt, and poured what remained of the water into the row of oil cans which contained the Lanaras flower garden. She whispered to Nicholos that everything was ready, then led them inside, where Father Lanaras and the schoolmaster were deep in conversation.

Though Roberto's hair was a shining masterpiece of brilliantine and overcombing, his eyes were bloodshot, and Nicholos knew that neither of the men was happy. The conversation broke off, and Father Lanaras turned from his old friend. He called Christo up onto his lap, and the boy went as though to his own father.

"Look here, Nicholos," said Roberto. "Did you by any chance take a shot at me this afternoon?" Nicholos stared at him. "Well, some young man rushed up to my window this afternoon and shouted, 'Forgive me if you wish!' and then fired a bullet into the wall over my desk."

"Who would want to do that?"

"Your father, for one," said Roberto, making a joke of it.

"My friend, I'm not that bad a shot," said the priest. His voice was too hollow to support the humor.

"Well, Serifos won't miss one bad schoolteacher," said Roberto. "But frankly, I'm worried. Things seem to be getting out of hand, with these fires and the men going out."

"After wolves," said Nicholos.

"I wish that were all," said Roberto.

"What did you expect, my friend?" asked Father Lanaras.

"Simply that Serifos would be vigilant. Ready to defend herself. I didn't want this madness."

Father Lanaras said, "Wasn't it you who once told me that it was better for a soldier to be too cruel, too savage, than to have too much human sentimentality? If a soldier is to be worth anything, he must be the exact opposite of a Christian man. I think that's how you put it."

"Very well, but I never counseled them to go out looking for trouble. It's madness! It's that Dimitrov."

"He's lost both sons."

"Shot one himself, and everyone knows it," said Roberto. "Rather than this insanity, I'd stand beside you at another meeting. You'll have my complete support, for what it's worth."

Since the last meeting, Nicholos had not heard the bell once and his father had vowed not to ring it again in vain.

"Haven't things gone too far?" asked Father Lanaras. He seemed almost reluctantly to gather his reserves. "Very well. We will ring the bell tomorrow. We'll try again."

Angela called them all to dinner. Bread, cheese, and olive oil seemed never to run out. Now that it was summer, there were figs and blood oranges from the south. Nicholos ate his bread heavy with oil; Christo clutched bread in one hand, cheese in the other, as though he feared the food would be whisked away.

When the meal was over, Father Lanaras invited Christo to spend the night, but the boy said he wanted to go home. Home? It seemed strange to Nicholos that anyone could regard a mud hut as home. But he couldn't expect fully to understand the refugees, who at first had kept to themselves with what seemed a guilty reserve toward the old inhabitants. Gradually they had begun to boast of the fine houses they had abandoned, the gardens and the olive plantations which never failed to yield, of luxuries Nicholos knew could not have existed in Greece even in the best of times. When asked about the atrocities they had endured, they became reticent, seeming only to recall the splendors that had never been. If they ever left Serifos, he wondered how they would remember the mud huts.

"I'll go with you," said Nicholos.

"It's dark out," replied the boy.

"It's a summer night full of stars," said Nicholos. "I'm going for the fresh air." He knew Christo did not like walking alone at night. No one did any more. They were all afraid, and seldom went outside after dark even in the heat. All life in Serifos was infected by the growing terror. Every unusual act aroused suspicion: the late stroller, the match struck in an alley, a shot high in the hills.

Nicholos left his friend on the edge of the refugee camp and, returning, acknowledged the sentinel's challenge at the barricade. He asked if the hunters were back, and the answer came, "Not until dawn." Outside his home he met Roberto. He nodded in passing and would have gone on had not the Italian clutched his arm. "Nicholos, a boy like yourself can be robbed of his youth in such times. That's painful, but it's a pain that passes. It's harder for your father, so look after him, do you hear? We'll see him through. . . ." They separated, but Roberto's voice came from the shadows. "This world wouldn't be worth saving if it weren't for men like him. That's the truth, Nicholos."

When Nicholos entered, Angela was reading and his father was writing letters in his old-fashioned schoolboy's hand. Even in her reading, Angela showed no looseness or relaxation. Father Lanaras looked exhausted. There was a touch of gray in his hair and in the black pointed beard, yet his father was not old. The face was still tanned and taut and dignified, as though he had finally come to grips with the problems he most dreaded.

"Yes, we will ring it again and again. Every day, if need be," he said. "Perhaps one day they will really listen."

Nicholos was not sure whether his father was writing aloud to the bishop or addressing one of his children until he said, "What do you think, Angela? Will mankind ever help his brother?"

"He will, Father, for a price," she said, scarcely glancing up from her book.

Father Lanaras scrutinized his daughter from under thick brows. "Perhaps that's true. We all desire something. . . . Do you think man can be liberated from the beast? What do you say to that?"

"What do you want me to say, Father?" asked Angela. "May God give you the answers." Nicholos knew she would not argue. She disagreed so completely with her father. He was not surprised when she left the room with an urgent glance, as much as to say, "Hurry, we have no time to waste." But Nicholos could not simply turn his back when his father wanted to talk. It was not through respect for the priest that he stayed, for he had lost much of that, but because he had come to love his father more than ever before. For the first time Father Lanaras seemed completely human and vulnerable, and Nicholos loved him with a sadness for what he had come to regard as his father's innocent desire to perfect mankind. He knew it was doomed to failure.

"Come here, Nicholos," said Father Lanaras. "I want to tell you something. Do I seem like a foolish man to you?"

"No, Father, of course not."

"That's strange, for I often do to myself. I wake up in the morning and ask myself, 'Why has God put me here? What am I to do?' "

"You'll do what is right, Father," said Nicholos, knowing he was slipping into formula.

"God has given me a strong body, Nicholos, and a spirit to match, I think, but he will not put them to use. Faith is a torment. It is like trying to please someone who is out there in the darkness, someone who never speaks, while every day the world conspires to prove there is no one there at all. This will sound presumptuous to you, Nicholas, but after your mother left us, I asked Him why I must suffer so much and accomplish so little. He suffered only three hours on the cross, while I . . . no, I'm speaking blasphemy."

"I think of such things in moments of weakness," continued Father Lanaras. "Faith is not easy to preserve in this world, and it is even harder to plant faith in others, harder still to restore faith when it has been lost. There is only one thing to do. Tomorrow we will ring the bell. We must try to convince them again that no one destroys in God's name. In each of us there is a wolf and he is a terrible enemy. All these centuries, and how little he has budged. How many of us still do his bidding. Tomorrow we will ring the bell, Nicholos, and every day. One day it will be up to you."

Nicholos nodded, not trusting himself to speak.

His father put his arm around Nicholos' shoulder and held him in a crushing grip. "As long as I have you," he said; ". . . I worry sometimes about Angela."

Nicholos worried about her, too. He worried more about himself, and what had become of his former confidence in his father's convictions.

When he climbed to the loft, Angela was waiting with

85

all the evident impatience of a coiled spring. Beside her stood a lantern and in its bug-swirled light he saw the Mauser rifle. His immediate reaction was that his sister looked like a beautiful and dangerous stranger, but he did not tell Angela that. He said instead, "You know, Father's concerned about you."

"About both of us, if he had any idea."

She was right, of course. Father must never know what they were doing at the old tank.

"But Angela, I think sometimes you deliberately try to make him unhappy."

"I know I do," she said, and began to pace the small chamber, her hands hugged in her armpits. She went back and forth, prowling like a predatory animal, and he waited for her to speak again. "Father and I see things differently, but there isn't time for that now. I'm afraid, Nicholos. I think we had better get the stuff out there tonight. It's those fires, and not hearing from Thanos that bothers me."

"Do you mean to leave the gun out there?"

"Yes."

"And ammunition?"

"Everything, tonight."

"Don't you think the children will find it?"

"No, they think the tank is haunted. They won't play near it any more."

"What makes you so sure?"

"I told them it was haunted. They believe me."

"Angela, I was wondering. Would it be all right if I told Christo?"

"Don't be silly. If we start telling everyone, what good will it do us? You've been listening too much to Father. You'll soon be as simple as he is."

"Maybe we need a few simple people. Look at what the sensible ones are doing." But, grudgingly, Nicholos agreed with her. He wanted to stay alive, and he had seen what happened to defenseless people. He remembered Stavro.

Angela lowered her head and her lips moved slowly as if she were spelling something out in her mind. "I don't mean all that about Father. I really don't. I love him too, Nicholos, but he doesn't understand." For an instant Nicholos expected his sister to burst into tears. Then she pushed the heavy brass shells one after another into the magazine and slammed the breach shut. "This little knob is called the safety. Leave it on," she said. "When you're sure Father's in bed, take it to the tank. I'll follow in a little while."

Outside the house, he took a deep breath. The roof had been exposed all day to the sun and the slates were contracting in the coolness with tiny explosions. Overhead, stars hovered so close they looked like moths about to bat their wings against his face. When he came to the sentry, he announced himself but kept the gun behind his leg. "Have you heard anything about the others?" asked Stratos. He had been at the barricade for six hours and he was tired. His voice had lost all of its bravado. "I wouldn't expect them back till dawn," Nicholos told him, and Stratos groaned and sat down.

Alone on the hillside, Nicholos looked once around. Nothing out of order. He made for the tank, ducked through the hatch, and groped for the stub of candle Angela had left there. Here was water, stale bread, blankets, and—most important—an impregnable fortress where they could hide in case the Andarte attacked Serifos. Here if need be they could defend themselves. Angela had already said the gun was hers. Nicholos accepted that, as he had accepted the marks of her growing on the door, always an inch or two above his own. But Angela would never use the gun. However ruthlessly she might talk, he knew that underneath she was gentle, like their mother; too humane to take life. He was not sure of himself any more. He had not been able to shoot a wolf and his father's pacifism was still strong in him, but it had been shaken by harsh realities; by the slaughter of the Andartes, by Stavro's murder. Outside the haven of his father's house, the world was a wilderness.

Nicholos stowed the gun and covered it with a rotting piece of canvas, because he did not believe Angela's ghost story was good enough to keep the children away. Why hadn't she arrived? Could she have been intercepted by Stratos at the barricade? He did not want to wait all night. There was going to be a storm. Heavy clouds were snuffing out the stars. It was eerie among the graves, and when he thought he heard footsteps, he dared not call her name. Instead he began counting silently, and when he had come to two hundred he decided to wait for her outside the barricade.

He hurried down the treacherous path, only to stop short at the sound of a half-forgotten cry. Far below it echoed, transparently thin yet terrifying: the cry of the Andarte. Then came a concussion that jarred the path under his feet and a sudden flame that lit the entire village. Tiny figures, darting from wall to wall, were revealed.

The schoolhouse on the edge of town was burning, and Nicholos ran until he stood in its red glare. A bright snow of sparks went whirling up toward the sky. There was nothing to be done there and he knew that he had to get out of the light. He never considered returning to the tank. He wanted to go home. In the street of the butcher shops it was quiet and dark, and he crouched behind a heap of crates. Just beyond there was a crowd milling about the chapel. All the women and children, all the old men of Serifos seemed to be there. Hemmed about by armed Andarte, they clustered around the chapel door where Father Lanaras stood so tall and strong that Nicholos wanted to cry out. Father Lanaras was trying to shield them all, and when an Andarte threatened him with the butt of a gun, Father Lanaras caught the stock in his hands, tore it free, and broke it on the stones. He did not fight and he did not budge. When another Andarte raised his gun to fire, Angela burst from the chapel and flung herself upon him. Nicholos could hear her voice over the crowd. He could shoot her down like a dog, she was screaming, but he wasn't going to touch her father.

From his concealment behind the crates, Nicholos could see it all. Serifos had been taken by surprise while most of the men were away. With virtually no resistance, the Andarte could execute their revenge.

Nicholos kept whispering to himself, "That's my father! That's my father!" for he expected at any moment to see his father killed. A great sob gathered in his throat as he ran toward the square. No one intercepted him and he easily broke through to the chapel, where his father still held the door.

"In this house there is still God!" thundered Father Lanaras, and his arms, his powerful body, blocked the door. Roberto was behind him, trying to persuade him to move, but it would have taken a bullet had he not grappled Nicholos in his arms. "Get behind me quickly," he ordered, but a hurled brick took him off guard, and he fell like a slaughtered ox. In the doorway he tried to rise, grasping the frame with both hands to pull himself up. Another blow brought him down and Nicholos fell on his father to keep him from being killed.

The Andarte began rounding up the children inside the

chapel. In the crowd Nicholos saw little Aphrodite and the Metaxas twins. Christo edged toward him and pressed his face against Nicholos' side. While they waited, the Andarte broke into houses, threw things from windows, set fires. A few tried to burn the chapel. It would not burn, so they kicked over the iconostasis and pulled together on the bell cord until the ancient bell fell clanging to the floor.

Its fall was a summons to order. A bearded man who seemed too old to be an Andarte shouted orders, and the children were shoved into groups. Some old people cried and cursed and threatened. Father Lanaras made no such outcry as he struggled to his feet and lurched to the center of the chapel. Unarmed, his face covered with blood and bruises, he seemed about to attack the enemy with his bare hands. On every side the Andarte awaited him. Nicholos felt a silent scream mounting in his chest, but his father attacked no one. He went down on his knees, embracing the great bell. There was utter silence as Father Lanaras tried to lift it, actually moved the terrible weight from the floor. Though hot tears blurred his vision, Nicholos did not move as slowly the bell slipped down. Once he might have risked his life to replace the Judas bell, but neither the bell nor his father belonged to the world he had so recently come to know.

Father Lanaras lay still, crumpled up, the bell still grasped in his arms. The Andarte began shouting orders again and Nicholos felt the pressure of the children behind him. He let himself be driven outside without looking back, for he knew his father was broken as the bell was broken, forever. He knew, too, that along with the children of Serifos, he was being kidnaped.

6

Nicholos had taken the road from Serifos many times before, but always with the prospect of a happy journey and an imminent return.

At first their progress was chaotic, with mothers clutching their children, screaming threats and being threatened in return. Finally the women were driven back, but their shrill voices rent the air with promises of revenge. The Andarte would not get far—if the men of Serifos failed, God would hunt them down.

Then it was stumbling down the dark path to the north road, where more Andarte with a shadowy train of pack mules were waiting. Here the children were grouped for travel, the youngest to ride muleback, the older ones to walk in column. Nicholos observed no haste on the part of the Andarte, no apprehension that the threats of the women might be carried out. Perhaps the Andarte felt invincible, yet they looked like ordinary men worn to the bone by the rigors of mountain life. Their clothes were rags. A few were barefoot, others shod with clouts or sheepskin. Some had stolen shoes from Serifos. Saddlebags were stuffed, loot was bargained, laughed and quarreled over, while Nicholos and the others waited.

Nicholos wondered about the men from Serifos. The sentinel had said they would not return until dawn, but perhaps they had heard the explosions. Perhaps they saw the fires; together with the forest fires they put a poison into the air which burned his lungs. Evidently the Andarte were concerned after all, for he heard a commotion from the head of the column, the sound of mules being whipped into motion. Commands were shouted. Ahead of him a boy no bigger than a jackrabbit rode backward on a mule. As the mule lunged forward, the child made the noise of a twanging bullet with his tongue. Then the mule was out of sight in the dark and Nicholos was walking after it.

For a short time they followed the north road, then a lesser road into the mountains. The pace was grueling, and some of the children began to cough in the smoke-filled air. A few cried. Those who were already refugees were used to suffering and, like Christo, were silent. Nicholos never let go of the little boy's hand. He stumbled now and then, his sight turned inward upon the monstrous pictures the night had printed into his memory. He kept seeing his father. He was not dead as Stavro was, but when he revived, when he understood what had happened, what then? His body would survive, but Nicholos felt his father's spirit would surely die. They might destroy Nicholos' body too, as Stavro's had been destroyed, but he made a vow: he would not be defeated while he lived. They would not take his soul.

Without warning, the Andarte stopped. Nicholos thought it was to allow a rest, but two heavily laden mules were led past him and on the trail behind him he heard shovels grating. It was not long until the rumor, passed from one child to another, reached him. The road was being mined.

Nicholos squatted in the dust, trying to rest, trying to breathe. He heard the wind rising with the coming storm. At least rain would flatten the smoke, but as the wind whined over the bare slope he began to worry about his flock. So far as he knew, they had not been taken by the Andarte, but left alone they would be helpless. He worried, too, for the men of Serifos, who would never see the fresh marks of shovels in the rain. Before they were again goaded into motion, he knew that he must try to escape.

With any luck he might slip away into the pitch blackness. A few yards from the trail he could safely hide or he might plummet blindly into a gorge. But the chance might not come again and he sent a message of readiness to every muscle in his body. Then, at the last, he did hesitate. He had completely forgotten the hand that held his hand. Strange how his hand seemed locked in Christo's as though his flesh did not want to do what his mind told him must be done. Christo would understand. He had only to explain, but words were hard to find. While he pondered, the fluttering of a match put an end to all thoughts of escape, for behind the sheltering hands holding the flame he recognized the face. He could see the teeth and the shadow on the nose thrown boldly up between the damaged eyes. Thanos walked just behind him, daring him to run. By the time he had moved away, they were on a path so sheer and bare of cover that escape was impossible.

Nicholos knew that Angela was somewhere ahead of him, unless she had accomplished what he had failed even to attempt. For some time he did not try to catch up, partly through fear of not finding her, partly because he thought

Thanos might still be watching. Then, over Christo's complaints, he increased his pace until he caught sight of her, walking moodily with a resentful, angry tread. He wanted to catch up and take her hand, but his certainty that her sympathy would not fail seemed the greater reason for not seeking it. He walked close behind, hoping she might notice him and speak first, but she did not and finally he said, "I suppose you know Thanos is with us."

"Yes. I hate him!"

It was difficult to talk because of the wind. The first shower had passed, but there would be more rain.

"Are you very tired?" she asked him.

"No."

"You sound strange. Have you been crying?"

"I don't remember."

She said, "I wish I could cry. I must have lost the knack." He couldn't remember her ever crying, when he thought about it. She always seemed too much involved in the present for regrets.

"You know we're going to escape," she said.

"Just the two of us?"

"It wouldn't be possible to take anyone else."

Before the killing of Stavro he would have argued with her. He would have thought of their escape as a kind of crusade, with Christo, golden-haired Aphrodite, even the Metaxas twins; all of them escaping together. Yes, he would undoubtedly have imagined them striding through kaleidoscopic fields of butterflies, singing hosannas. How naïve he had been! But he was too tired to despise his old self, too tired really to think. Anyway the path was too narrow now and too steep for escape, and Angela seemed content to bide her time. As if to belie her hidden intentions, she began encouraging the others. Nicholos resented her vivacious leadership, and the feeling shamed him. She carried a six-year-old on her shoulders, held another by the hand. For all of them, Angela was a pillar of strength, and it seemed easy in his weariness to follow her commands.

Nicholos felt the first drop of rain on his cheek, and he extended his loose jacket around Christo's shoulder. The child must be half dead from walking on his scarred feet, but he did not whine or complain. He had found the person to whom he belonged, and this was a trust Nicholos could not take lightly, no matter how selfish he told himself the world really was.

Slowly at first, and steadily, the rain began to fall over Macedonia. In the valleys and low hills it fell as rain, and in the high mountains it fell as sleet. Where the children walked, it came first as one and then the other, and Nicholos held tight to his companion's hand for fear he might stray. Together they followed Angela.

7

From a soiled gray sky occasional showers fell, and Nicholos hunched his shoulders. He was bigger and sturdier than most, and he had solid shoes. Many were barefoot or shod in sheepskin, plodding through the half-frozen muck. At least the small ones were allowed to ride mules. Behind him rode little Aphrodite, her worried face as white as flour. She looked like a defeated angel. All of them did.

While they marched and during the frequent halts, Nicholos kept Christo with him. He was only beginning to discover how tough his young friend was. The Metaxas twins, Yamris and Lias, didn't seem to mind either. Stocky gargoyles to look at, they had forever played at war, and Nicholos imagined they were the sort who might willingly become Andarte. He had never admired the pair, except for their impressive trick of whistling between fingers and teeth, but he respected them now for their jaunty stride. He wondered how long they could keep up the show. And Angela . . . how long could she walk with a child on her shoulders? How long could she sing that way to the little ones? After a while she stopped singing and no child rode, but she held one by either hand and he heard her counting steps for them— twenty-five to the fallen tree, fifty more to the jutting root. He found himself counting silently. It helped, just as it used to help when he had cut his finger or scraped his knee and his mother had said, "Count with me." They had counted to ten repeatedly, and every time they reached ten the hurt would be less.

At dusk they made camp and food was portioned out. Nicholos ate squatting in the mud. Others straddled wet stones or clung to the backs of mules, while the Andarte set up makeshift tents. Nicholos crept into one and tried to submerge reality in nostalgic dreams of the old days of innocence, but even in this way he could not escape. When he tried to re-create lazy hours with his flock, he saw only Ajax, basting on the Andarte's fire. When he conjured up his father dancing in the village square, he saw him instead crumbled on the chapel floor. And Nicholos knew that, no matter how hard he tried to repudiate his father's beliefs, part of himself lay broken on the tiles. In his mind, he tried to raise his father, tried to re-establish him in the chores of daily life, but Angela's whispering destroyed the picture utterly.

Her voice was full of urgency. Within a few days she expected they would cross over into Albania and be interned. The alternatives were either escape or initiation into the Andarte.

"You don't mean you'd really become an Andarte?"

"I mean to pretend," she said, "until we have a better chance to escape."

"They'd know we were faking," he said.

"Plenty have joined them, just like us."

"They make you take some kind of blood oath, don't they?"

"So what, Nicholos? If we can get out of this with just one easy lie we'll be lucky."

That was true, but his word had always meant a great deal. It seemed a part of his soul.

"What will become of the others?" he asked.

"Internment."

"And after that?"

"Nicholos, how should I know? Sure, I'm sorry for them. If I had any luck to spare, they could have it, but I'm doing all I can right now. They're too young for Andarte, and too young to escape. They'd die. They're better off in Albania. That's the truth."

It was true all right, everything she said, but he still felt like Judas Iscariot surrendering all those innocents to a godless exile. You've got to look after yourself or you'll never get home alive, he told himself, but he could not look at Angela's face because of the excitement he knew was there. He could not think of his father without being filled with shame.

"The thing to do, Nicholos, is to be friendly and interested. It's got to be gradual, as though we're thinking it over. Not all at once—that wouldn't seem real."

"What do you want me to do first?"

"Leave it to me. I can get people to do whatever I want." By *people* he presumed she meant Thanos. There must have appeared some vivid comedy of dismay in his face, because Angela laughed. "Don't be gloomy. We'll both be all right as long as you remember not to act like Father for a while. Trust me, Nicholos."

He always had, but when Angela was with Thanos she was not herself. Then he was not fond of her either. She was a stranger, as she had been at the Fire Festival when she'd worn her mother's fancy clothes and had gone out to watch the boys jumping over the bonfires. She'd gotten Thanos to build one up, the biggest bonfire Nicholos had ever seen, and coaxed him to jump over it until Nicholos had expected the jumper to emerge all in flames. She was making Thanos build it still higher when Father Lanaras had come and taken her home by the arm. What a terrible look she had given their father! Nicholos couldn't forget it, and the way things were working out it probably would have been better if Thanos had been allowed to burn up, there and then.

"Don't go bothering Thanos," he said. "We don't need him."

"He can help us," she said. "Don't you see? He's so stupid, he'll believe anything I say."

That was the end of their conversation. The camp was settling down into exhausted sleep. Only an occasional sentinel moved as the sky went black and the deep valleys disappeared. Nicholos lay on muddy straw and listened to Christo's heavy breathing. He tried to blot out the present with thoughts of the past, of birthdays before the war, of Easters and holidays, but he kept coming back to Angela and Thanos. So many of his earliest memories had to do with them. One of the earliest and most shocking concerned Thanos alone, and some summer crickets which he had collected in a cardboard box. Thanos had called them "father crickets" in what Nicholos remembered as an affectionate voice. Their hopping had sounded like the tapping of a tiny drum. Then Thanos very slowly had pressed his foot upon the box until it was flat.

Remembering that and other cruelties, how could he let Angela go to Thanos alone? For a while it seemed as though she would not go. The moon had risen and he was about to give way to sleep when a dark shape passed beside him. It was Angela. Nicholos rose and followed. He heard voices before he saw them, and he hung back in the shadows. Thanos was standing guard in the moonlight, and he could see clearly that Thanos had been wounded again. A fresh scar ran from one corner of his mouth along the jaw, and a thin growth of beard did not conceal it. He heard the two of them laughing. Nicholos knew Thanos for what he was, and he knew too that Angela would use all the weapons at her command to prepare their escape.

"I like men who aren't afraid to fight," Angela was saying.

"Come on, what is it you want?" demanded Thanos.

"Must I want something? I only thought you might be lonely out here by yourself."

Nicholos watched, confused and resentful, while Thanos put his hand on Angela's waist and let his fingers creep around.

"I don't like that," she said.

"Why come tempting me?"

They were so close together Nicholos could see only one silhouette. "That's enough! I'm warning you!"

Thanos seized her hair in one hand. He gathered it around his fingers and pulled her toward him.

To Nicholos it was like the touch of a razor. He rushed at them, only to stop short as Thanos turned on him, so quickly that he must have been prepared.

"Ah, the mascot! I thought I'd flush you out. What's the idea? Trying to gang up on me and get away? That your idea?" said Thanos, but his voice was not vindictive. Rather it seemed to Nicholos a weary voice, that of a man too long at war. "Come ahead, I'm not going to shoot anybody. Sit down, Nicholos. Make yourself at home."

Nicholos did as he was told. Despite the favorable reception, he did not trust Thanos. "You were my brother's best friend. I don't think you'll make it home, but I won't stop either of you if you want to try."

"Was it because of Stavro . . . what happened to him . . . that you attacked Serifos?"

Thanos dug the butt of his rifle into the ground. "Do you think I'd have burned my own house if we'd found the ones who killed him? Stavro hardly knew how to hold a gun, and they shot him down."

"Don't you know who did it? Everyone says. . . ." Too late, Nicholos realized his mistake. Thanos half-rose, his face so close that Nicholos could feel his breath.

"Who? Tell me who killed my brother!"

"There are only rumors . . . nobody knows. . . ." Hands were tightening on his throat, thumbs pressing together. Nicholos hated those hands, and he wrenched away. "It was your father!" he shouted vengefully, and immediately despised himself.

The change in Thanos was appalling. He slumped down limply, as though his backbone had been extracted. His lower lip was drawn into his mouth, and he must have bitten it for he spat something dark onto the ground. Then he rose and pointed his gun. Its muzzle was on a level with Nicholos' belt buckle. "That's a lie," he said.

Angela leaped for the weapon, but Thanos swung it so viciously that she fell. With a terrible animal cry, he brandished the rifle over his head. Nicholos flung himself upon the Andarte, and sent the gun clattering, but when Thanos didn't go down, he knew he was in for a fight. Thanos

101

inserted the fingers of his right hand into a set of steel rings. Nicholos' arms were long enough to avoid these weapons for a moment. Then Thanos lunged and hit him in the chest, beside his nose, pushed him away, and clubbed him twice behind the ear. The earth began to slide and Nicholos found himself on hands and knees. He was kicked in the side and rolled over. As he struggled to rise, he heard Angela screaming, "I'll kill you! I'll kill you!"

Nicholos did not know whether she meant him or Thanos, but it was Thanos she struck with a stone. Thanos sat down, holding his head, and for an instant Angela stood poised above him, still holding the rock. She hesitated, cocked her arm for a final skull-splitting blow, then she let the stone fall as there came the crack of a rifle bolt being drawn, and a stranger's voice commanded, "Stop or I'll fire."

Tough and gnarled as a mastiff, the captain of the Andarte stepped into the moonlight. His sleeves were rolled up, revealing massive arms and hands holding a carbine.

He jerked Thanos to his feet. "You all right?"

"I'm all right. Just leave me alone," was the sullen reply. The captain stared at him until Thanos, his eyes averted, added, "Sir."

"Thank you," said the captain. "Now get back to camp. I've a job for you in the morning."

Angela bent over Nicholos. "Are you badly hurt?" she asked.

"I don't know," he muttered. Expecting at any moment to be sick, he did not want people around.

Weary and graceless, the captain sat down on a boulder beside him. He supported himself with an outstretched hand. Old for an Andarte, there was a tracery of pink veins above his frosty beard. It was apparent to Nicholos that he was in no hurry and intended to talk.

"Did that fool break anything?"

"No," said Nicholos, but the captain persisted. "Let's have a look at your teeth." With thick fingers he tried to pry open Nicholos' mouth. "How old are you, boy?"

"Sixteen," Nicholos told him, adding one year for some reason not clear to himself.

"And I'd say you weigh around a hundred and thirty pounds. What did you want to fight him for? Didn't you see he was wearing those things? Was it to escape, boy? Was it that? Or maybe the girl. Is she your sister?"

Here Angela helped him out. "This is my brother, Nicholos." She went on to explain about the fight, the Dimitrov household, and the suspicions concerning the murder of Stavro.

"Thanos always did strike me as queer. Now I understand," said the captain. "Well, you don't have to worry about him any more. I've got a message to send up north. He'll take it . . . you seem like a fighter, boy. You both do."

"We can look after ourselves," said Angela.

"Have you ever thought of joining us? Many Andarte are younger than you, and you seem to enjoy a scrap."

Suddenly and unexpectedly their opportunity had arrived. Angela would have snatched at it, but Nicholos was no actor, and he had never entirely welcomed the idea. "What would we have to do?" he asked.

"You know the Klephts, the palliars of the songs? We're like them, only updated; living off the land, fighting to free Greece. Some call us brigands, but soon we'll be welcomed as liberators."

"Yes, but what would we have to do?"

103

"To begin with, nothing exciting. Minding mules, cooking. Eventually some responsibility, some fighting. Besides an oath, we have ways of testing loyalty. We've many dependable comrades like you. Some of them have been elected officers, and you'd be amazed how many women have joined. It's a better life than internment in Albania, believe me."

"Do you think you can trust us after the way we were forced here?"

"We can't trust anyone at first."

Nicholos looked at Angela for her reaction. "It's what we both want," she said.

"Do you know how to use a gun?" asked the captain.

"Yes," said Nicholos.

"And kill a man?"

"Yes."

"You don't sound very sure. Well, we'll be visiting Psarada tomorrow. We'll find out there."

"Isn't that near Yugoslavia?" asked Angela.

"Yes. At the foot of Monastir by the frontier gap," said the captain.

"I thought Psarada was burned out months ago."

"It was," said the captain, "but they built it up again."

"I met some people from there," said Nicholos. "They were peaceful and friendly."

The captain studied him. "There are no peaceful or friendly people. We're at war in this country. One of our men was hung at Psarada. He was a fool, and he deserved it, but if someone chips your tooth you have to smash out his entire jaw. If you want to win a war, that's how it's done . . . all right, I've got to get back. Can you get up?"

"Don't worry about me," said Nicholos, but when he got

to his feet they seemed a long way off. His legs felt dead, and Angela gave him a hand. The captain supported him from the other side; for a big man, he was extremely gentle.

The captain left them at their tent. Nicholos had not been encouraged by their changed circumstances but Angela seemed exhilarated, like a mechanical toy wound too tight. First she upbraided him for attacking Thanos, then she threw her arms around him and kissed him. "Why did you have to get yourself beaten up? I thought he'd kill you."

"You almost killed him," Nicholos said.

"Why did you do such a thing? He had a gun."

Nicholos was not sure of the true answer. That Thanos had knocked Angela down was only the last straw. From the moment those hands had touched Angela and she had seemed to like it . . . from that moment, Nicholos had wanted to hurt Thanos.

"We're lucky, Nicholos. The captain likes you. . . . I could see it."

"Smashing out other people's jaws," said Nicholos disgustedly.

"I wonder what we'll have to do to make them believe we're sincere."

Nicholos was too upset for further conversation. He lay down on his side, facing the canvas, but the Metaxas twins had evidently been listening and they crawled over, full of questions. Yamris was the spokesman for the two and Lias had an annoying trick of imitating him. "What's going on?" asked Yamris. "What are you talking about?"

"Nothing. Go to sleep," said Nicholos.

"I heard we were going to attack a village tomorrow."

"Yes, we're going to attack a village," echoed Lias.

105

It annoyed Nicholos that they should both use the word *we*.

"We're going to attack Psarada," said Angela.

"Someone told me they overheard the Andarte talking about Psarada becoming a base. How we were going to bury ammunition and guns there for safekeeping until the army goes away in the winter. Then we may attack Florina," said Yamris.

"Florina?" said Angela. "That's practically a city."

"That's right," said Yamris. "They need a city. They'll call it 'Free Greece' and invite the Albanians and the Bulgarians to send troops. That's what I heard."

"Is it true, Angela, that we older ones will be invited to join the Andarte?"

"Yes, it is," she told him.

"That's terrific!" Yamris was obviously intoxicated with heroism and eager for great exploits. "That's terrific, isn't it?"

"It's better than prison," agreed Angela.

Nicholos wanted to be alone. He wanted to sleep if possible, so he got up and crossed to the far side of the tent. There he lay with his knees pulled up and his hands locked around them. Behind him he heard whispers. "What's wrong with him?" asked Yamris. Angela began describing the fight with Thanos, and after a while he did not hear them any more, though it was some time before he slept. His face hurt, and under one eye a swelling beat like a second heart. There was tomorrow to worry about: his masquerade as an Andarte, and worst of all the oath he would swear against God. In his father's eyes, he would be joining death's army, one with those who denied God and worshiped violence. Not that the Andarte seemed so individually vicious. His feelings about

Thanos were a personal matter, but the others seemed like ordinary men under their grimy masks.

Hardly had his eyes closed, it seemed, when Angela was shaking him. There was light in the sky and the camp was awake. It was tomorrow. And the day began much as the days that had gone before, with marching and talk that died from weariness. All day they kept going until it seemed they must have bypassed Psarada. Then toward evening they stopped on a ridge overlooking a quiet town. From where Nicholos stood among the stunted carob trees and the wild prickly pear, paths twisted like pale veins showing through the tawny hide of a great lionskin, down to the town called Psarada. Here the Vlach shepherds, the wild men of the stories, led their goats; here farmers toiled under silvery olive trees. Here a priest must ring a bell like the Judas bell. It was like every town he had ever seen: stony, clinging to the steep hillside as though it clung for life. This was pine-forest country, and the houses were probably wood, not mud bricks or stone as they were back home. He would know when he saw them burning.

Nicholos kept his back to the Andarte, most of whom were working over their weapons—cleaning, loading, loving them. If it weren't for the metallic chatter of metal on metal he might have been at home, on his hillside above Serifos. He could even imagine the smells: olive oil, and goat, and sweet fermentation, for the grapes must be in the vats by now. Then he noticed something out of the ordinary. At the far end of town there appeared black figures scurrying, forming into a procession with banners, also black. He saw trucks, too, on the valley road. That must be the way to the Monastir gap and the border. If it were not for the low-lying clouds, he might have seen the fabled mountain.

Just as the Andarte seemed about to fall upon the village, the attack was called off. Nicholos whispered a prayer of thanks, then learned it was only a postponement. The trucks, it seemed, were from the United Nations, and the black flags were part of a demonstration in behalf of the kidnaped children of Greece.

"Do you think they'll talk about us in the UN?" asked Nicholos.

"Of course," Angela told him.

Nicholos was impressed. He watched the trucks, praying that they would not leave, and when darkness fell they were still there. Lights came on below, though the Andarte camp remained dark and cold. He imagined he smelled sausage frying with onions, and his mouth watered. The old men of the town would be gathering at the coffee shop, drinking ouzo from tin cups, smoking narghiles and chibouks and making up verses about their neighbors. They would have no idea of the fate that hung over them, no idea; nor would the mothers, singing nursery songs of Drako and Saint George. Then he remembered the black flags. The children of Psarada were already gone. His thoughts tormented him, and throughout the night he scarcely slept. The braying of a mule announced the dawn. The Andarte were once again toying with their weapons, and the trucks had gone.

Nicholos watched the village as it came to life. A donkey began turning a great wheel at the olive press. Thick smoke billowed up from the olive grove, reminding him even more of Serifos. Farmers were drugging the wild bees to start a hive, and he remembered the taste of the wild mountain honey: lemon-flavored, sharper than the honey from Hymettus.

Finally the lieutenants started down with their men.

108

Nicholos made no move to join them, but the captain found him and any chance of being left behind vanished. From the ridge they crept through the first small plots of onions and tomatoes, keeping behind the plaited-cane walls. On closer inspection the town looked tired. Stone and timber showed through paint like the cankerous skin of old lepers. Some houses were boarded up, others burned-out shells. Painted mustard yellow, red, and—for patriotism—blue, night shutters were still closed. People must be still asleep. In the cobbled streets sparrows pecked and chittered. With drowsy regularity the chapel bell began to ring and Nicholos could almost see the priest who rang it, innocent of human savagery as his father had been. Then a dog barked with rising inflection, and a man in a red apron emerged from a doorway, peered at them, and bolted back inside with his wide shirt sleeves flapping.

"All right, comrades!" shouted the captain. The Andarte began running toward the center of town as the village bell peeled hysterically. A shot was fired, and someone beside Nicholos grunted and fell. Then the Andarte closed in. They began entering houses and throwing grenades. Psarada had no chance, and as Nicholos watched, the citizens were driven into the streets, down to the main square. There were no children, only women and a few old men. House after house was ignited. Nicholos felt as though it was his own town that burned. The eyes of the captives, wide with horror, seemed to plead with him from faces bronzed by the flames. A woman repeatedly thrust out her fingers in the sign of the evil eye. She pointed directly at him, and all he could think was "I deserve it . . . I deserve much worse for what I am doing." In the old adage, the priest's son was the devil's grandson. That was right. He wanted to slink away, to hide, never to be seen again. He wanted to tell the woman that he was helpless too, but a false move would at the very least mean internment, possibly a shot in the back.

Nicholos lingered helplessly until he felt a hand on his shoulder. "Come along," the captain told him. "There's one last job."

He found himself trudging in a squad of eight. The Metaxas twins were there, faces smudged, eyes glittering in the flames. The group halted at the edge of the village where a hummock of earth reared behind the chapel.

A rifle was handed to each member of the group; to each one, a single cartridge. Delightedly the twins worked the bolts, thrusting the shells home.

"Get going," said the captain. "Get that thing in there."

Nicholos opened the breech.

"Hurry up," the captain commanded. With trembling fingers Nicholos laid the shell in the breech. "Now close it." Nicholos shoved the bolt forward and down.

They were formed in line and told to wait. Presently two Andarte appeared, hauling a third figure who did not seem able to stand. Nicholos saw that it was a man of middle age with an expressionless face who was dragged before the mound of earth. Since he could not stand, a chair was brought and he was forced to sit on it.

Nicholos' flesh, muscles, stomach, registered faster than his mind. A terrible contraction seemed to squeeze all the moisture in his body out through the pores of his skin. This was the test. He was part of a firing squad.

The village priest was hustled roughly forward. Nicholos experienced an odd sensation of relief when he did not look like Father Lanaras but was short and elderly with a ruff of feathery beard. He was allowed to pause before the prisoner.

His words were too faint for Nicholos to hear, but he saw the silver cross held up. When the cross touched the victim's lips, he opened his eyes as though it had brought him to life. Then the priest was led away and commands were shouted, rifles were raised and aimed. Nicholos could hardly hear what was being said because of the buzzing in his head. He was about to take human life. He was about to swear an oath to the devil, to death. . . . Flames leaped from the rifles and the prisoner spun from the chair and landed on his knees. Slowly he fell backward, bending at the waist with his face turned up toward the sky.

The man was not dead. He lay panting and dying. Nicholos felt a scream rising in his throat. What had they done? Oh God! Vaguely he saw the captain walk to the prone figure, bend over with a black revolver close to the man's left temple. Nicholos closed his eyes.

Something violent happened inside his body, an eruption over which he had no control. Nicholos began screaming and beating his rifle on the ground, trying to break it as his father had done. The gun would not break, and hands grasped him, pulling at him. He bit down on one of the hands. Then he fell, and it was his own bleeding hand between his teeth.

Dimly he heard voices.

"Look at this. The gun's not fired. There's a live cartridge in the breech."

"Lucky he didn't use it on us."

"I think he's gone crazy."

"All right," said a familiar voice. "Get up! Everything's finished here."

The captain sat beside him like a rock in the poor light. He took Nicholos by the hand and guided him back to camp, but there was no talking between them. Nicholos knew that he had failed the test, and he was glad.

For some time nothing was very clear. He saw faces, heard voices, rejected food someone shoved at him. He tried to sleep and could not. Then Angela's voice cut at him like a rawhide whip.

"You fool! Why did you have to do that?"

At first he didn't understand. What did it have to do with her? Then she told him because of what he had done the captain had decided to send them all to Albania.

"What difference did it make? All you had to do was shoot. He was killed anyway."

"I couldn't."

"You could have shot into the ground at least."

"You wouldn't have been able to do it either," he told her, but Angela assured him that she would have aimed for the prisoner's heart. That was the only humane and sensible thing to do. Nicholos loved his sister too well to believe her. He knew that she could not kill another human being.

"What will happen now?" he asked dully.

"As soon as they bury the arms, they'll march us off to prison. I would rather be an Andarte forever than that."

He looked around. The camp had been pitched in a depression above the town. Where great boulders leaned together there was a natural arch, a cave entrance into which the Andarte were carrying boxes.

"For the attack on Florina?" he asked her.

"Of course. But by that time we'll be in Albania. If you weren't a complete fool, we might have been able to warn them." Even if she were right he could not regret his conduct. He would let her talk, say anything about him she liked without contradiction. That way her fury gradually

112

subsided. Finally he put his hand gently to the back of her neck and said, "We're together. We'll be all right, and some-day we'll all get away, all of us."

She turned on him, and her lips were trembling. "Will you leave me alone? Can't you see I want to sleep?"

So he left her, and lay down beside Christo. The child gave him a smile with no subtlety behind it. Here was warmth and honest friendship, the last person in the world who seemed to need or want him. He was sorry for Angela, but he was secretly relieved for himself.

For a long time Nicholos could not sleep. Beside him, Christo stirred. The moon etched out the child's small face in cameo. "We're both pale and thin," thought Nicholos. "He might be my younger brother." To have pulled that trigger would have meant forsaking Christo, and the others. It would have meant sacrificing his own integrity, all that his father had ever taught him. He felt that he had made the right choice though in a day or two they would be interned in Albania, perhaps never to see Greece again.

The moon and the stars spread a silver radiance in the sky that turned a harsh and ugly land into a place of beauty. Cold as it was, the distant lights seemed to warm him. After a while he was not thinking clearly any more. He was driving sheep—or was it children? The images merged. He sensed there were wolves on every side, but he could not see them. They were swarming toward him and he would have to fight them all, and kill them. He was glad he did not have to kill the moon and the stars.

8

Nicholos stood at the end of the line. Because of the snow he could not hear the tread of soldiers' boots before the dreary sentry boxes. There was only the clatter of tin plates. Snow fell in a swift screen blotting out footprints and turning his companions into ghosts. It lay heavily on the corrugated tin roofs, disguising them, but the tarpaper walls stood out from the snow, Bible-black, spaced with the regularity of prison bars to remind him of where he was.

Nicholos was hungry, but he did not hurry. Sometimes he skipped meals altogether. At other times he shared his portion with Christo.

How long had it been since that day their bedraggled procession had arrived? In the tedium of routine, time had lost substance. One morning the dormitory supervisor had informed him that he had been in the so-called Red Cross hostel for three months—September, the month of the vintage and the cross; October, Saint Demetrios' month; November, the time of sowing. All had passed, yet it seemed as though the same day had been going on since their arrival.

What frightened Nicholos most was that presently he would not care. Red Cross hostel, prison, indoctrination camp, whatever one chose to call it, the place seemed to be changing him. In the early days he had been troubled by the ways and thoughts of a free man. He had hated the damp, the narrow crowded room, the thin walls that did not keep out the wind. Now his thoughts were becoming prisoner's thoughts, the routine was becoming his life. The fearful march, the sack of Psarada were episodes in a dream, though he vividly remembered their arrival in this soulless camp. It had been a haven at first, with a flush toilet, and a shower shooting hot water out of a dozen nozzles. He had never showered before, but had stripped off the remains of his clothes like soiled bandages and had gone under the hail of scalding water. There had been few such showers since, and the feather mattresses they had heard about had turned out to be straw. Then the straw, too, had disappeared because it bred lice and typhus. But Nicholos was used to hard beds. It was not the beds or the food that he really minded, and not even the lessons. No one had to believe the lies they made up about Greece and the King, though some of the children seemed to. Nicholos did not want to be a mechanic, nor after his experience at Psarada could he imagine himself even as a counterfeit Andarte. These seemed to be the choices; these or doing nothing at all. He had been locked away from a world where shepherds were needed. This, and concern for his father, had kept Nicholos resolute in his intention to escape.

When he reached the head of the line, a ladle was emptied onto his plate. He accepted its contents wordlessly. There was a joke that the bull-necked little cook was really a magician, and that he filled his black cauldron with strange herbs and slimy things found under stones. But it was always there, twice a day, and many of the children could not honestly say they had been better fed at home. Nicholos sat down under the eaves and Christo sat beside him. Christo did not eat, but thrust his hands into the new snow like a baker molding bread. Nicholos told him to eat if he wanted to grow.

The stone-and-timber houses of the little town were dressed up in snowy hats and plumes. There were furrows through the snow where people walked. He thought it must be a nice town at Christmastime, if Christmas was celebrated here. In class they kept insisting there was no God.

For a long time Nicholos had had no idea where they were. Psarada had been near the Yugoslavian border, but they had not gone through the Monastir gap. He had studied the village signs through the wire fence, and Angela had stolen a classroom map. The village was Pogradec, and she had located it in Albania very near the border of Yugoslavia. They were not so far from home as Nicholos had thought.

Though the children from Serifos were housed in one building, he had seen little of Angela. Long and narrow—a shotgun building he called it—the dormitory was divided down the middle by a thin partition: girls on one side, boys on the other. Common ground was the bathroom, which was unlocked alternately onto either wing; here Angela and Nicholos could meet. When the place was open on the girls' side and the supervisor was not around, Angela had a way of inserting a sheet of cardboard under the latch to the boys' side. The trick did not work in reverse, and they had to be careful. Otherwise they met only during meals and periods of exercise, and when they were together, they discussed escape.

Angela talked of "you and I." All along her intentions had been the same, but Nicholos spoke vaguely of "us." Did he mean by that all the children from Serifos? Even within himself he wasn't sure, but he knew one thing. His experience with the Andarte, the memory of his fallen father, had shaken his confidence in Angela's opportunism. When alone, he saw them all marching home, to the smallest child; but when he encountered Angela, all his fancies added up to nothing concrete. She planned only for the two of them. "I don't mind taking the others," she had said, "if you will guarantee a miracle. Something like a pillar of fire and smoke to lead the way. Otherwise, it's got to be a secret between us." Nicholos did not argue this discrepancy in their thinking. He would go away, disappointed with himself, to spend dull hours lying on his stomach, tracing outlines on the floor with his fingers, striving for a moment of illumination. Instead of plans, vague visions came. This was Crusader country. Peter the Hermit had passed this way a thousand years ago, and that was how he saw them all returning, like a Crusade, with banners. Occasionally his mind turned to something more practical—to ladders and heavy wire clippers and shovels to dig underground. But they had none of these and the ground was iron-hard, the fences high. They had no money to bribe a guard, but still he knew they would get out somehow, through the enemy, over the highest mountains. The autumn passed while Nicholos calmly dreamed out his dangerous dream.

With winter his imaginings seemed less feasible, and it was easy to wish that the snow would never stop. All of nature might be completely smothered, and no spring would come to test his dreams against Angela's reality. All responsibility would be buried in the snow. Already it lay inches deep and was still falling. Each flake was a feather; the feathers fell thickly and the guards no longer tried to brush them from the trucks. Now the windows were black and shuttered against the cold, and smoke rose from the camp's banked fires. The days of December, Saint Nicholos' month, passed quickly. Back home, the Karkantzari with their red faces and excreting mouths would be roaming the streets, doing mischief. The doors would be locked against them, and the houses would be warm with roaring fires and rich with the buttery-sweet smell of Christ's cake. With the renewed faith in his father's humanitarianism had come the belief that he had survived his terrible beating. Nicholos pictured him raising the Judas bell, summoning the village to communion on Christmas morning with its sound. For a moment he seemed to hear the bell. Then the wind whipped the melody away, and Nicholos plunged his hands deep into the pockets of his goatskin jacket. Even there they were not warmed.

Presently Angela came and sat down. Aphrodite was with her. She was always with Angela, as Christo was with him. The little girl looked healthier than he could remember. Angela pulled Christo's hands from the snow. She forced both children to eat, and they did so automatically, like sausage grinders. Angela put some of her own food on their plates.

"Listen," she told him. "I have some real news. I'll tell you in private." She drew him to his feet and they walked along under the icicled eaves. "Nicholos, I've found a way out." As he listened, she described a means of escape which in its simplicity seemed alarmingly possible. There was a window in the lavatory, shuttered, but held only by a weak latch. Since the first heavy snow the sentry post below this window had been abandoned. Yugoslavia lay no more than eight kilometers to the west, and there was a persistent rumor

118

that Tito was no longer helping the Andarte. Once over the border, they would be as good as home. "We can make a dash for it any time. No supplies or anything. What do you think?" At first he couldn't think at all; his body simply needed to move about. "Well, think about it. . . . We can go tonight!" That was how Angela did everything—suddenly, and with absolute conviction that he would accept her decisions. Even knowing this, he could not have been more disconcerted had she dropped a scorpion into his lap.

"Shouldn't we take more time?" he said. "Shouldn't we put some food aside and wait for a good night?"

"There aren't any good nights," she told him.

"What about wolves, Angela? I've heard there are wolves let out at night to guard the camp."

"That's ridiculous. There were dogs before the snow came. Listen, I've got hold of an old white blanket and I've cut it up into capotas. No one will see us day or night."

"What if we get lost?"

"Don't be afraid, Nicholos. I'll find our way by the stars."

"Suppose it begins snowing. Hard."

"All right," she said. "I'll find a compass."

"But you haven't one now," he said triumphantly.

"I don't understand you, Nicholos. In a little while they'll be carting us off to Siberia. We'll never get back. We'll be slaves for the rest of our lives. What's really the matter, Nicholos? Are you afraid?"

"No, it's not that."

"Then stop biting your nails." She pulled his hand away. "Look at them, Nicholos. That's a baby trick. You'll give yourself blood poisoning."

"Angela, I'm not afraid, it's only . . ."

"Only what? Why so many objections?"

"I can't go without the others," he admitted finally. "I used to think that I could, but I can't. Do you understand?"

"Of course I do, but it won't work. Besides, do you seriously think they would want to go, even if they could go all the way in a truck? Let's try something—" Christo and Aphrodite had been watching, and when she called they came like eager puppies. She put her arm around the little girl, who attached herself to Angela's skirt. "Is the food good here, Aphrodite? Do you like it? You'd rather stay than walk home over the mountains, wouldn't you?" Aphrodite answered yes to all these questions.

"Ask her if she'd like it here without you," whispered Nicholos, but Angela only repeated the original questions to Christo and got the same response. "Go along and play," she told them. "I've got some private things to say to my brother.

"All right, Nicholos. They've been told everything is good here and they believe it. They've copied letters home saying how lovely the place is." When Nicholos reminded her that Christo had no home, she said, "Well, the others have. You've seen those letters they write in class, all about soft sheets and eating better than Greek children and not hearing American bombs. They believe it!"

But Nicholos had made up his mind. "If we leave them here," he explained, "they'll be taught that God is dead."

"Isn't He?"

"They'll be trained to kill Greeks, Angela. We can't let that happen."

"Nicholos, if you have such a tender conscience, think of the children in Florina, and what the Andarte will do to them. If we get away, that may be prevented. Look, I know the way you feel! But how do you intend to feed them all? How will you keep them together?"

He could not answer these questions, and there were others he wanted to ask Angela. Why was she so determined to get home? She had never loved Serifos or their father as he had. What would she do if they met Thanos again? He could not forget the two of them together in the darkness, but these were inquiries he dared not make.

"See," she said, "you haven't answers because there aren't any." With this she fell silent, awaiting his solution as one might a magician's impossible trick.

"We have to try, that's all."

"How?"

"Just try. Your conscience wouldn't let you run off any more than mine would. You couldn't leave Aphrodite. Every one of them is devoted to you, Angela."

They had been speaking as breathlessly as though their struggle were physical. The icy air in Nicholos' lungs cut like a knife. Now he waited as Angela took a long breath. She looked down at her hands. "Nicholos, I'm not as hard as I try to seem, but I've always been practical. When there is something you want to do, if you know it's impossible, forget it. No matter how much you want it, concentrate on the next best thing. There's no use being sentimental. You can die of that." She looked at him sadly and forced a smile. "We're not getting very far, are we? Do you imagine you can get on any better without me than I can without you? You're right about the compass. I'll get one somehow. If we can save up a little food, a few of the older children can come with us. It would be too hard on the little ones. They'll have to stay for their own good. If that sounds all right to you, we can make some real plans."

121

As abruptly as she had begun the conversation, Angela broke it off. The meal period was drawing to a close, and she urged Christo and Aphrodite to finish what was on their plates. Nicholos watched her with amazement. She obviously cared for Aphrodite. She was treating her like a little sister, and still she could calmly plan to abandon her along with the others.

Aphrodite made a grotesque effort to swallow, but the muscles of her throat tightened and an expression of disgust flushed over her face. "Spit it out, then, but remember that people who are enemies of food don't live long." Aphrodite spat out the repellant cud, while Angela scraped the food she had failed to eat onto her own plate.

Presently the bell rang, and the children were herded back to their dormitories to make way for another group.

Over the land snow continued to fall, deep and dry and sifting through chinks in the walls. It became so deep that Nicholos ceased worrying about escape. Angela showed him a compass one day, and a small crowbar, but with the sky still falling into a white eerie world, these tools seemed completely useless. The branches of trees beyond became so great they snapped. Others sprang back, shedding their burden in silent explosions of glistening flakes. Doggedly Nicholos marked the passage of days and weeks. January passed, the month they called The Pruner. February came, the damp month of illness his mother had called the vein-sweller. The snow grew old and became trampled and flecked with soot, and then there appeared the first pockmarks of rain.

Nicholos no longer slept well. Soon they would be going. Angela told him to save whatever imperishable food he could find. There remained only this task and the selection of those who would go with them, when something happened that threw their plans into confusion. It came about exactly as Nicholos had pictured it in a moment of depression, with the loud knocking and throbbing of a motor in the courtyard. Nicholos heard the sound, and did not have to press his face to chinks in the shutters to know what made it. They were diesel trucks, the sort the Germans had used in the Hitler war.

First one, then a crowd of boys had gathered to peek through the chinks in the shutter. At first he ignored the excitement, but when it did not subside he joined them at the window. It was dusk outside, but standing on tiptoe he could make out the huge motor vans in the courtyard. Children from one of the other dormitories were climbing aboard. As the first van moved, it swung very close to the window. Nicholos could see near the roof a small open panel which framed four or five faces. At the corners of the panel gleamed terrified eyes. Some of the mouths opened, but the cries were wordless or drowned by the motor. Then the van was swallowed up by the night.

Nicholos knew nothing more until he met Angela in the lavatory. She had an explanation. For weeks there had been the rumor of a UN inspection team on its way, and to prove that there were no hostages being held in Albania, the camps were being emptied. Within a week this one would be deserted. They would all be on their way to Hungary, and those who went would not come back.

"What will we do, Angela?"

He could still see those faces in the van, imagine his own screaming wordless mouth pressed against the chicken-wire grille.

"It's a mess," she told him. "The snow's too deep and we

haven't any food, but it has to be tonight, Nicholos. And it has to be our secret."

"Shouldn't they at least know what's going on, so they can decide for themselves?"

"Shut up and listen," she said. "We haven't much time. Tonight, as soon as it's pitch dark, come to the lavatory. Put on the heaviest clothes you have. Steal, if necessary, but remember! Come alone!"

For Nicholos the intervening hours were a torment. This was not going to be his way. This was not the dream he had nourished through long hopeless weeks. Their father would never have given up. He would never have deserted his congregation, no matter how terrible the prospects. When Stavro had died, defenseless, he had decided his father was wrong about life, and Angela right. But with the firing squad, he had made a discovery about himself as well. At first, the memory had been so horrible he could not recall it in detail. It had been simply a time of blinding, searing light. Now months had passed and he knew this. Never, however great the expedient, could he cold-bloodedly drive death into a beating heart. Nor could he forsake these children without something inside him being broken. He had believed in his father's humane world too long to cast it aside entirely. Even if it were madness or a fool's dream, it was part of him and he must somehow match his dream with the facts of the night to come. If only he had Angela's intelligence and his father's strength. If only he could be like the eagle, circling on great wings, dominating the heights, fearing nothing. But he lacked the courage and the intelligence to command even himself.

Finding no solution, Nicholos wanted to blame Angela for all that was about to happen, and because this wasn't just, he blamed her all the more. It did no good to tell himself there was no other course. The least he could do would be to prepare Christo with the truth. There would be others to tell him lies once he had gone.

"Christo," he said gently. The child came happily, like a pet expecting a caress from a beloved master. He sat on Nicholos' lap. What was he to say now? Christo's face became puzzled. When Nicholos finally opened his mouth, the words that came were not those he had intended.

"Christo, why do I always have to be responsible for you?"

9

The windowpanes were as dark as the dormitory room itself. The day was finally spent, and Nicholos moved cautiously toward the washroom door. He managed to affect an indifferent saunter, but his thoughts raced ahead.

He went like a blind man, his left hand touching the outer wall. Through cracks in the wood he felt the night wind stirring. Finally he located the door to the washroom, found it ajar and entered. "Angela? Angela?" he whispered, but received no answer. The window was a gray patch in the blackness, and it was open. Against the outer wall Angela was waiting, calm and impersonal, as though this adventure would cause not a ripple in her serenity. But there was a tidal wave to come, and Nicholos could no longer hold it back. The first hint was a small boy's voice, turned to full volume, then another angrily silencing him.

He had confided only in Christo and a few of the bigger boys, but in a crowded dormitory he hadn't really expected the secret would be kept. He had not honestly wanted it to be. Within moments the news had spread excitedly. It might have reached the guards as well, had not the building been sealed for the night. At first he had been glad and excited too, and then he had begun to worry. They didn't seem to comprehend the hazards involved. He had tried to explain, but for most of them it was a lark, and all he could accomplish in the end was to quiet them down. Now, with the Metaxas twins helping, he pushed them one after another through the window. He dared not contemplate Angela's reaction and he tried not to count. Certainly more than half of the boys had decided to come. When he found himself lifting Aphrodite through the window, he realized the news had spread across the corridor. Either that, or Angela too had weakened. In any event the choice had been offered and he felt suddenly clean, as though his whole body had been scrubbed inside and out. Joyfully he swung the last small figure over the sill and vaulted lightly through himself.

Angela stood silently, her hands raised to either side of her face, slowly shaking her head in growing comprehension. Nicholos tried not to look at her but she came to him and took hold of his shoulders. By the way her fingers stabbed through his jacket he knew she was full of fury. Her voice hissed softly, "You can't do this! No, you can't!"

But he had already done it.

"You've ruined everything, Nicholos! Why, after we had an understanding?"

Nicholos deprived her of a scene. "I'm an idiot," he admitted. It was no time to argue, and Angela must have known it. Given the circumstances, he knew she would sort them out and make the best of it. In terms of logic and good sense Nicholos had messed things up, but he knew with even greater conviction that this was the only way of escape for him. He felt as if his old hesitant self had been sheared away, and henceforward his every act would respond to the dictates of his conscience.

A far-off sound drove them against the wall. From the sentry shed, a beam of light crept across the icy ground, explored the fearful instant like a snake, then disappeared. They had been lucky.

"Let's go!" whispered Nicholos.

Angela squared her shoulders. She had accepted the inevitable and started off at a trot. Nicholos followed her with the others. There must have been twenty or more, and he was giddy with exhilaration. Only the weight of his shoes seemed to hold him to the ground. At any moment he would fly off the earth's surface. He felt indestructible. If Angela faltered or despaired, she would find out what reserves he had. For the first time, no part of him rebelled. He was acting wholly in accordance with his father's faith, his own faith revitalized. No matter what, he would keep going, without food or rest, without stopping. He would carry them all on his back if need be. He would lead them through the high mountains when Angela became exhausted.

In the shadows of the first house, Angela stopped. The others grouped around her. "Listen carefully," she whispered. "I have a compass in my hand, and I know how to use it. If you think you can't keep up with me, go straight back to the camp. The rest of you can try to follow, but I'm not looking back. We have no food, so keep your eyes open as we go through town." She started off quickly, then turned and faced them again. "And be quiet! If you don't do exactly as I tell you, none of us has a chance."

Nicholos brought up the rear as they stole through the main street of Pogradec. With any luck, they would make it to the Yugoslavian border before dawn, before the alarm was sounded. He wished it were darker, but the sky seemed very low and was filled with shredded clouds through which a full moon sailed unsteadily. Nicholos dug his heels into the icy ground, but this did not prevent him from slipping. Some of the children fell down. He helped them up and encouraged them, urged them on. None must get behind him and he kept looking back not so much for signs of pursuit as for fear one of them might have strayed.

No dogs barked. No voices issued from buildings until they passed the village tavern. There it was slushy underfoot and a street lamp burned red in the frosty air. From inside came the noise of glasses and tongues, and the cold windows were steamed over from breathing. Music struck up, and as it did, one of the smallest children walked toward the door. Perhaps he was cold, or hungry, or tired of games. Whatever the reason, Nicholos was too late to head him off. The door opened and the child entered. The laughter stopped, then the music. Nicholos prodded the others. It took all his restraint not to run ahead. But no crowd poured into the street behind them, no shouts of alarm pursued them. They neared the edge of town. The last street light made the frosted cobbles glitter like millions of tiny diamonds. There awaited the empty darkness, and they plunged into it.

With Pogradec behind them, Angela called a halt. Some of the small ones wheezed from exhaustion. A few already wanted to go home. "That's where we're taking you," Nicholos told them, but they meant the camp, and he knew it.

"It's too late for whining," said Angela. "Did anyone find food? Nicholos?" She turned to the Metaxas boys. "What about you two?"

Not a voice responded.

Something heavy was thrust into Nicholos' hands. "It's a

129

cheese," said Angela. "I found it hanging outside a shop. It will do for a day or two."

Nicholos took the cheese and slung it from his shoulder.

Angela started moving again. Nicholos helped the littlest children to their feet. The Metaxas twins were nearly as old as he was, and he appealed to them to watch the flanks of the ragged procession for strays. Grudgingly they agreed.

Fortunately Angela's pace was slower now. She carried Aphrodite on her shoulders, and her frequent stops to check the compass gave the others a chance to catch up. Only during such pauses did Nicholos see her. She was so sure and erect beneath her burden that he longed to catch her by the shoulders and say. . . . He wasn't sure what he would say, but she seemed more splendid now than she had ever been. As long as she was there to lead the way, as long as he was behind to rescue those who lagged, they would be all right.

"I can't run any more!"

It was Christo. Nicholos urged him to hurry up. "Never lose sight of me for a minute!" But he felt guilty. From such a lapse Christo might have been lost altogether, and he cautioned himself to be more vigilant.

"I can hardly see you any more."

"Here I am . . . here's my hand." But a hand was not enough for Christo, and Nicholos carried him. Christo's legs drew tight around his neck so that they seemed more one body than two. "Keep your hands out of my eyes!"

"I think we're being followed," whispered Christo.

"Don't be afraid."

"I mean really followed."

"I've been listening, too," said Nicholos, "and I haven't heard anything."

130

"I saw things, like shadows. They weren't making a sound."

"The moon and the clouds make shadows."

"These shadows are following us."

"Don't be silly!" Nicholos' voice was hearty, but his imagination was aroused. They were involved in a monstrous game. They were the hiders with the night to hide them, but somewhere the seekers waited while an invisible clock ticked off the seconds. Soon would come the final ticks. Ninety-nine, one hundred, and the seekers would begin their deadly hunt. Children of the folk tales had magic on their side, combs and needles that turned into nails and thorns to slow their pursuers; but darkness was *their* only protection, and under its cover insignificant things became terrifying. Nicholos' own shadow, enlarged by Christo, darted and crept along in the glimpses of the moon, over rocks and frozen bushes. He seemed to hear the seekers already. "Don't look back," he told himself. "They may be gaining." If nothing more, the monsters of his imagination were close behind. His body moved disjointedly. He informed his legs what to do, his arms. He advised all the sections of himself in those dreadful moments.

"Look! Don't you see them? Out there!" said Christo.

Nicholos saw nothing at first, until the shadows caught and held his gaze. They were moving with that jolting yet effortless stride he knew so well.

Wolves! A she wolf and her litter were traveling cross-country. No killer pack, he felt sure, and yet all his instincts urged him to run. Even more than the creatures of his imagination, he dreaded the wolves. His knees seemed no longer willing to support Christo. A shepherd had told him that wolves feared music, even whistling, but his mouth was too dry to make a sound. "Can you whistle a tune, Christo?" he asked. With the first shrill note from the child's lips, all the shadow forms stopped short, fixed for an instant, and then flowed away. Christo laughed aloud, and Nicholos took a long slow breath. This time he'd kept his fears, imaginary and otherwise, to himself, but he realized now that wolves would be prowling the unsettled land through which they were bound to pass. There, where the flocks had already been ravaged and the packs were starving, a whistle would not turn them away. There they would not distinguish a child from a lamb.

With the disappearance of the wolves, the night passed uneventfully. They walked and rested and walked and never seemed to progress until they came at last to a body of water. Large and silvery, Lake Ohrid stretched before them. Nicholos knew that part of it belonged to Albania, the rest to Yugoslavia. He had no idea, nor did Angela, whether the border would be patrolled. They could not be sure until they found a border station or a Yugoslavian town called Ljumanista that showed on Angela's map.

Along the banks of the lake, streams of melting snow presented new hazards. They all managed to leap across the first stream, but the second was wider and Angela stopped.

"There's ice in the water," whimpered Aphrodite.

"There would be," said Angela bitterly. "There would be every miserable thing tonight."

"I'll lift them across," offered Nicholos. He turned to Lias and Yamris for help but Yamris said he wouldn't risk frostbite for anyone. He leaped across the stream and Lias followed him.

Nicholos alone stepped into the water which rose around his ankles. Lumps of half-submerged ice floated, clear as jellyfish, in the moonlit water. The water seemed first to drive needles into his feet, then to lay hold of the bones themselves, but he kept them planted there until the last child had been swung across.

The next stream was wider still, and deeply swirling. Nicholos searched for a bridge. The one he finally found was old and fragile. Water sucked around its pilings and streamed away in deep whorls. They crossed fearfully. Nicholos went last, with the timbers thudding and swaying beneath his numbed feet. Beside the human prints, the moon etched out the clover-shaped tracks. Had the she wolf and her cubs passed this way, in flight themselves? For the first time, Nicholos felt a kinship with the wolves.

With Christo again on his shoulders, he followed the little troop. Each stream crossed, each bridge, was another barrier against pursuit. Though numb to the bone, Nicholos experienced a joy and pride he had never known before. Nothing could stop them now.

Toward morning it began to snow lightly. The trail they had left would quickly vanish. Nicholos' muscles were so tired they had stopped hurting, and he had to look down to make sure his feet were still there. That was a bad sign. Occasionally they cramped under him, and remembering the frostbite casualties from the Hitler war he was apprehensive of what he would discover with his socks rolled back. More soldiers had fallen from frostbite than from bullets, and his father had made an appeal to the congregation for roller skates. From these platforms could be made for cripples who otherwise would not move at all.

Nicholos squinted into the half-light. They would have to find shelter soon, but snow lay everywhere except on the lake, which drank up the flakes. There was no sign of the

133

wolf pack or of human life. Then faintly he heard the jangle of a church bell. At the sound, Angela stopped and turned around, a confusion of emotion on her face.

"What's the matter with you?" he asked. "Are you laughing or crying?"

"I'm laughing and crying. . . . Are you deaf? Don't you hear?"

Suddenly he knew. East of Pogradec only one town touched the lake: Ljumanista. They were over the border, beyond patrols, and as safe as they could hope to be on this wild journey. The others made no show of rejoicing. They were stupefied and brute-tired.

Angela refused to risk visiting the town, but in this war-ravaged land there were plenty of abandoned structures. Nicholos had no trouble finding a stone fold dug back into a hillside. From his own experience he judged that it was situated in a summer pasture which would not be used for months to come. With the crowd of small bodies packed inside, it became warm rapidly, a thick furry warmth that made the air taste twice-used. Someone began to cough. Nicholos did not like the sound of that, but soon everything was quiet and they slept. He alone was awake, free to see them with objective eyes, free to wonder what it was in himself that had brought them here. Most of them were children he scarcely knew. Some were the children of neighbors, the rest were refugees known to him by sight or name alone, and yet his life and Angela's too might be forfeit because of them. As they lay helpless in sleep, he loved and pitied them. Waking, as they soon would be, he might come to hate them all. They might well hate him before this trip was done. These were questions for time to answer, and he needed sleep, but the physical anxiety of his body would not allow it. Blood thumped in his ears and his feet were still numb. Frostbite led to gangrene, and he saw in his memory legless veterans pushing themselves on the roller-skate carts. He sat up, feeling sick. Gingerly he pried off his shoes and socks and rubbed his feet with snow until the circulation began painfully to return. The agony assured him his feet were alive. They were not rotting under him yet, and he lay down again.

In the darkness he listened to the breathing of his companions, and to one in particular. It sounded as though the sleeping body were carrying a weight with terrible effort up a steep slope. The breathing broke with a cough, began again laboriously. He could tell in the half-light that it was Aphrodite. Angela was awake, too, holding the child in her arms, crooning softly a song he remembered, giving comfort as his mother had done years before. He pretended it was for him, but it was hard to pretend. His eyes ached. When he tried to close them, they seemed propped open with matchsticks. He lay on his back with his arms crossed on his chest like a corpse. The song was over. Aphrodite must be asleep. He longed for sleep too, but thoughts forced their way into his consciousness, and were so real he lived in them. In his dreaming there came the call of wolves. Or were they tracking dogs? Had the clock finally ticked one hundred? Were the hunters coming at last? He wanted to warn Angela, but sleep bound his tongue and consciousness shouted its warning only in the deep recesses of his brain. There his thoughts were trapped, and he led the children over the same path again and again. But in his dreams they were not ragged and dirty, they were beautiful, and they carried white banners stitched with gold thread. All the children of the world seemed to march gaily behind him. He would not fail them.

10

From the color of the light filtering into the fold Nicholos knew it was afternoon. The others were still sleeping. Christo was on one side of him, Angela on the other. He could feel Angela shaking. This was the first hint he had ever had that she could be afraid. As he watched her, she gave a great start.

Hastily Nicholos counted the group. There were twenty in all, with Angela the oldest, then himself and the Metaxas twins a year or so younger. Four or five like Aphrodite were little more than babies. Gradually they were beginning to stir, the movements of one being communicated to the next.

Immediately Angela re-established her authority, demanding their attention. She was going to divide the cheese equally, she said, "And that's all you will have until tomorrow. So chew slowly and remember to swallow, no matter if it tastes like somebody's big toe. It's good for you."

All who ate seemed revived, but Aphrodite still slept. Her hair looked tangled and dry, like the fur of an animal that has died in the sun. When she finally opened her eyes,

Angela said, "Good afternoon, Aphrodite." She placed her hand on the child's forehead and said that she was much better. Nicholos knew that could not be true, and later Angela told him the girl had a high fever. Because of this and the late hour, they decided to stay in the fold until the following morning.

Nicholos wanted to reassure the children, but it was Angela who succeeded, by telling stories, rolling serious, savage eyes. She was a treasure house of tales which she brought out to make them all laugh. "This is where it's good," she would say. "Listen carefully." Nicholos gazed at her with reverence. She seemed radiant, as if she had looked into a crystal ball and found its promises good. She was the old Angela again, all he had ever admired, sure and sympathetic and strong. She laughed her old laugh, with her head thrown back, and it seemed to Nicholos there had never been a time in his life without her laughter, nor could he imagine such a time in the future. Her good cheer was contagious. Staring at one another through the gloom, they laughed until Nicholos had to press his hands against his side. The little children giggled themselves into a state of helplessness, and every burst of gaiety was a confession of the fears they dared not face.

As she had initiated the fun, Angela dispelled it, admonishing them to rest in preparation for an early start. Like a well-trained flock, they settled down. Nicholos listened for the breathing to become regular. It was only then that he and Angela could make plans for tomorrow. Not that he would have much to say, but at least he could balance off the Metaxas twins. After their irresponsible behavior at the stream he did not know why Angela included them. But there they sat, grinning like jack-o'-lanterns, with their eyes and big seed-corn teeth showing in the gloom.

"Everyone's asleep." Angela's whisper startled him. "All right, you three . . . come here to me." She produced her map, and matches with which to examine it. In the fluttering light she traced two possible routes, south around Lake Prespa or north by way of Monastir. Either way there would be Andarte and mountains and snow. "The Prespa way is shorter, but. . . ."

"If it's shorter, let's go that way," said Nicholos. It was around Monastir that the wolves were most to be feared, if one believed the tales. It was there, too, that Thanos and his band had their base.

"I was about to say," said Angela, "that going south around the lake will put us back into Albania for about twenty kilometers."

Even to Nicholos this was unthinkable, and the others agreed. There was no choice. They would have to go north, toward Thanos and the Monastir gap, which Nicholos thought of as the lair of the white wolf.

"We'll be near Florina, won't we?" asked Yamris.

"If we're lucky."

"And the place where the guns are hidden?"

"Probably."

"Don't you think we can get help right here?" asked Nicholos. "After all, we're in Yugoslavia."

"Maybe," said Angela. "But just because the Yugoslavs hate the Albanians doesn't mean we're going to be popular. Besides, what can they do about getting us home? They haven't automobiles, probably no mules; certainly not any they'd give away."

"We could steal mules," said Yamris.

138

Nicholos tried to ignore him. He said what they really needed was food and medicine.

"We can steal that, too."

Angela told Yamris to shut up. "The thing that worries me," she said, "is what to do about Aphrodite. She won't last long this way. The little ones haven't a chance on foot really."

"I'm not abandoning anybody."

"Of course not, Nicholos, but these people will look after them. No one, whatever their politics, can turn away sick children. If we even had some almond milk for her. . . . It's food we need most."

"My brother and I will steal some tonight," offered Yamris, and Lias grinned his approval.

Nicholos opposed stealing emphatically, but Angela turned to him. "We may have to steal." Her look seemed calculated to make him feel very young and foolish. "We'll have to survive like animals."

"But we're not animals, Angela."

"When it's a matter of life and death we are. I'm afraid the rest of us are not tormented by our principles at the moment. A priest may see the ways of God in a flock of sheep, Nicholos, while a wolf sees only mutton. They're both right, you know, but we had better all accept the wolf's point of view."

"You can thank God we've come this far," said Nicholos.

"You can thank me," said Angela, "and this compass. You really are terribly innocent, Nicholos. If you met a wolf and he leaped at your throat, what would you do first?" She was deliberately provoking, and he did not answer. "You'd pray, wouldn't you? Would you pray for the wolf or yourself?"

"For heaven's sake, Angela, shut up!"

He turned a threatening glance upon the twins and their smiles hardened, but the silent rebuke seemed only to spur Angela's sarcasm.

"Your old friend Saint Francis would have prayed for the wolf first. Where do you think we would be now if it had been up to prayer?"

Though Nicholos was annoyed, he did not believe she meant it all. He was willing to let it pass as an outburst of the tension that gripped them all.

"I can't get you mad, can I?" she said.

"Not this way," he lied. "It's a waste of everyone's time, too, don't you think?"

"You're right," she admitted. "Anyway, we know where we're going. All we have to do is find out if the Yugoslavs are friendly."

"And get food," added Yamris.

"Nicholos and I will go into the village tomorrow. If we're lucky, we can find out about both things then."

"We can steal food now, while it's dark," persisted Yamris.

"That would be a fine way to find out if they're friendly," said Nicholos, and for a change Angela supported him.

Yamris was silent, but Nicholos did not trust his expression.

"Let's not talk any more. We should all get some sleep," said Angela.

The twins crawled away to a corner, talking in whispers Nicholos could not overhear.

"I'm sorry I picked on you in front of them," said Angela. "I'm jumpy. Don't pay any attention to me, Nicholos, and don't be angry. Try to rest. I'll wake you when it's time."

Nicholos lay down. He was annoyed with Angela and that made him angry with himself. Their only hope was to trust each other. They could not afford dissension. What was the defect in himself that let anger in? Was he jealous of his own sister? Did he want to make the decisions himself? He was not like his father, built for leadership, yet something inside him wanted to lead. These thoughts went spiraling away as he felt himself growing warm. It was surprising how warm a fold could be when it was filled with life. Only the emptiness in his stomach kept him from slumber, and then it too was dimmed. Nicholos slept, to waken suddenly with a pain in his leg. "Frostbite!" was his first horrified conclusion. He reached for his leg, but instead caught Yamris, who had stepped on him in the dark. "You!" he shouted. "You're not going off stealing tonight!" But Yamris and Lias had already been. Flushed with success, they proudly displayed two great pots of *yaourti,* the milk junket on which isolated shepherds lived for months.

"No one saw us," said Yamris.

"So don't make trouble. We took a big risk," boasted Lias.

Angela admonished the pair in such a lighthearted manner that it seemed to Nicholos more of a commendation. "Remind me to thank God for this good meal," she said sarcastically, a comment she must have immediately regretted, for she added in a repentant tone, "Did you sleep, Nicholos?"

"Well enough," he told her.

"You're still angry about what I said last night."

"Why should I be? I'd forgotten about that." And he really thought he had.

141

While the others were eating, Nicholos stepped outside. It was piercingly cold. The sky was still dusky but there was the smell and feel of morning. He watched a new star clearing the eastern horizon. Angela would have known its name, but he did not. The March wind blew steadily in the false dawn, punishing his hair. Then the sun appeared with a fierce onrush of light. A fine day was coming. The rushing sky above him opened, leaden, blue and white, with dazzling blades of silver and gold. Perhaps it was the pure air from the snows before him, perhaps it was the rich *yaourti* inside him that made him feel suddenly vivacious, inexplicably happy and at peace with himself. They were on their way, all of them. Possibly this day would see them safe. The prospect was as dazzling as the blinding sun rolling up from the horizon.

Abruptly he was conscious of someone behind him, and turned defensively. It was Angela.

"You look very happy all of a sudden," she said.

"I am. I feel I could do something wonderful."

"A miracle? We could use one."

"I wish I'd been able to walk on water the other day."

"Maybe one day you'll do a miracle, Nicholos. Sometimes you look like a mystic. No, really, I'm not teasing. When I came up beside you just now you kept staring off into space."

"I guess the weather has me in a kind of trance," he said uneasily. "Look at the mountains . . . all gold and silver."

"You should have seen yourself. You looked right out of an old icon—like an angel."

Though Nicholos took this for a compliment, it made him uncomfortable and he tried to make a joke of it. "If I were an angel, I'd ask for it to be warmer in paradise today."

"We're going to get home. I feel sure for the first time." She kissed him joyfully in the ancient manner, on both cheeks, then quickly went inside. They were over the border, and at worst there lay before them a tedious walk down a road Crusaders had taken hundreds of years before. In his mind's eye he could see it stretching away, a ribbon of silver toward the mountains, toward home.

He turned to follow Angela, then stopped at the sight of tracks in the snow, so fresh that the sun had not dissolved away the crisp edges. Wolf prints. Had the pack stayed with them then? He had heard tales of wolves following armies to feed on the slain. How could wolves sense a thing like a battle? Did the smell of death cling to an army? To them? He shivered in the morning cold. His father would not be afraid, he told himself; nor could he indulge his fear, for it would infect the others. Carefully Nicholos obliterated the tracks.

Hunched over, he re-entered the fold. There Angela was cradling Aphrodite in her arms. "We'll bring you hot broth," she promised. "Just you wait."

The sick child's breath came hard and rasping, and her eyes did not seem to focus readily.

"Yamris and Lias will look after you while we're gone," she told the child. As far as Nicholos was concerned that was like being guarded by a pair of snapping turtles. Still, what else could they do? When Angela went outside, he followed her.

With a brisk stride, they started toward Ljumanista.

"She's awfully sick," said Angela. "I don't want to guess how sick. Pneumonia, maybe. If we were home, we could use suction cups to draw off the fever. But in this place. . . . We've got to find someone to look after her."

143

"If we get some hot food, she'll be all right," replied Nicholos without conviction.

"She needs days and days of warmth and good food, or she'll die. She won't get that with us."

The problem seemed insoluble, and they did not talk about it. Ljumanista still lay a mile away in a landscape as pitted and bare as the surface of the moon. Neither the harsh setting nor the gravity of Aphrodite's illness could entirely suppress Nicholos. In a few moments they should have food, perhaps a pair of dry shoes for his feet, medicine. The worst seemed behind them.

"Smoke from the chimneys!" he cried.

"Not so loud," said Angela. "And remember, we don't know anything. We're a couple of hikers. We've never heard about prison camps or Albania."

Drawing nearer, he could distinguish a number of scattered dwellings with garden patches, and farther on a main street and a church. They approached the first farmhouse. Smoke curled and uncurled from its chimney. It was a frame building, with a balcony along one side and overhanging eaves. Only the whitewashed walls suggested Greek influence. Under the eaves sat an old man. His cheeks were brown and shiny and his mouth looked ready to laugh. His nose was a beak with the skin stretched so taut across its bridge that the bone showed whitely through. He was watching them intently. Angela hailed him, and at her call he half rose. Nicholos could see him more clearly as his face emerged from the shadows. He met eyes which, like the mouth, were laughing, but the laughter was as cruel as that of a child who had grown up in the wilderness.

Angela explained that they were on their way to their own village and had lost their way. She asked if they might

144

warm themselves. The old man listened with his head slanted toward her. When he replied, the words seemed as gutteral and formless as the gibbering of an ape. Even though the mountain dialects varied greatly, Nicholos was taken aback. The old man might well be telling them to go away, but hunger and their need for help interpreted the strange sounds as words of welcome. When a woman appeared on the doorway, her red cheeks and wide smile dispelled all his doubts.

She wore a white headdress and dark skirt, and her bosom was gathered into a baggy bodice with drawstrings at the waist. It made her look like a large, loosely furled sail. For a moment she conferred with the old farmer. "My husband says he has a hard time understanding you, but he believes you are hungry." Nicholos understood this, for it was the Slavic speech of Macedonian shepherds and bound by no national boundaries. He was quick to reply affirmatively. "Of course," she said. "Of course." He thought it odd the way she talked, hardly opening her mouth. It seemed no more than a crack across the face of a statue, and he decided she must have bad teeth and did not want to show them.

The woman ushered them inside to a low dark room where hay forks and harnesses, sausages and white onions hung from pegs in the wall. Nicholos felt immediately safe, in spite of the uniform that hung beside the hay forks. He was about to explain to their hostess about the others who needed feeding, when Angela put her hand on his wrist. He held his tongue, though he did not like being secretive with such hospitable people.

The woman began talking about food. She talked as though she wanted to see how long it would take for their

145

mouths to water. Nicholos already felt the roaring of his own saliva and his stomach had begun to contract.

The old man kept kneading his hands together and nodding at what his wife was saying. Finally she told him to help her in the kitchen, and he followed her through the door.

"I don't like this," whispered Angela, when they were alone. "Why doesn't she at least ask us where we're from? I don't like that woman."

Nicholos was astonished. He liked the woman very much, and said so.

"That's just it. She seems too good to be true. Why are they both so anxious to feed us? Why? They can't have much to spare. . . . Did you notice the uniform?" Nicholos nodded. "It's got the skull and crossbones on the sleeve. The old man was probably with the Chetniks before the war. That doesn't necessarily mean anything, but I don't like it."

Let her worry unnecessarily if she wanted to. Nicholos could hear the splutter of fat in a pan, and that was enough. After what seemed an interminable delay, soup appeared. The woman carried a huge bowl of it in her well-scrubbed hands. The mixture was disappointingly thin. Nicholos had to stir it constantly to keep a fair blend of water and vegetables, but it was hot and there were beads of fat floating on the surface. There was hot cider, too, which burned all the way down.

"Good?" asked the woman. "There's more. . . . My, you must have come a long way. Look at that boy eat!" Here she laughed with her entire face. The eyes disappeared in a thatch of wrinkles and her teeth appeared. As Nicholos had suspected, they were yellow and snagged and fitted loosely in her jaw. After watching her guests for a few moments,

146

she went to the kitchen and returned with a platter of dough fried in lard. Nicholos ate and drank at the same time and he began to sweat from the hot food and the strong cider. He heard nothing, thought nothing, except the feeling of the food as it slid down to his stomach and began to relax his aching body.

The farmer had not returned, but the woman sat and watched them, chewing her gums as though impressions and ideas were being sorted and organized by the working of her jaws before they took form in her mind.

"Going far?" she asked.

"Home," replied Nicholos. "How far would you say it is to—"

"To Monastir?" intruded Angela.

"Oh, a good day's walk over rough country," said the woman. "Longer if you lose your way."

"We've a compass," explained Nicholos.

"Ah, a compass? May I have a look at it?" Angela put the compass on the table. "Looks like an army compass."

"It was," said Angela. "It belonged to our older brother."

Nicholos looked at her, perplexed. They had not discussed this invention, and he wondered if she had had too much of the cider the woman kept pressing on them.

"I'm surprised. You live in Monastir, and all along I thought you were Greek. You certainly don't sound like the people around here."

"We're shepherds," said Angela. "We speak the mountain language as you do."

"That's what I mean," replied the woman. "You see, I am Greek by birth . . . and I thought . . . well, now and then Greek children pass through here running away from the camps."

147

"What camps are you talking about?" asked Angela innocently.

"Come now," said the woman. "Everyone knows of the camps." Here she made an effort to refill both their cups with cider. Nicholos put a hand over his. "For the poor refugees who have been rescued from the American imperialists. We have many such shelters."

"Our family was Greek, too," said Angela, "but they came to fight with Tito. Our brother was killed fighting by his side."

Their hostess was obviously taken by surprise.

"He was on a raiding party from Vis, and that Italian seaplane, the one they called *Giuseppe* . . . it. . . ."

"*Vis!* Holy Mother! I was there. *Partisanka Zena Clynick,*" said the woman enthusiastically. Then more soberly, "I'm sorry about your brother."

"It was a long time ago," said Angela, letting her eyes drop melodramatically.

"Perhaps I knew him," said the woman. "What was his name?"

To Nicholos' amazement, Angela replied, "His name was Thanos . . . Thanos Dimitrov."

"No, no one by that name," the woman said musingly. After a short silence, she leaned forward and looked Nicholos in the eyes. "Isn't it queer? I thought at first you came from one of those camps. If you had, you'd be foolish to cross the mountains this time of year. A person would only be doing his duty to help you back."

"Back home?" asked Nicholos.

"Back to where you came from . . . but of course you two come from Monastir and that's not a bad walk when you're young."

148

The conversation had taken on the tone of examination. The woman was spreading traps, and finally even Nicholos knew it. He was on his guard now, but against what he was not sure. "Come, let's be honest. You had better tell me, or I shall think it much worse than it is. For instance, I might think you were part of that bunch that broke away from Albania. . . . You look surprised. There have been many inquiries. But as you say, you live in Monastir. Would I have bothered to feed you if I intended turning you in? Tell me the truth."

That was sensible, thought Nicholos. A torpor was overwhelming him, a torpor born of strong cider and hunger suddenly satisfied. He did not want to think evil of anyone, but his suspicions were kept alive by the caution in Angela's voice. Something was passing between the two females which he did not comprehend. He saw Angela's eyes growing larger and darker, or perhaps it only seemed so because of the surprising paleness of her face. Suddenly his amazing sister turned the interrogation about. "Why is it," she asked, "that you are so interested in what we've been doing?"

"My dear, I'm naturally curious. . . . Would you care for more cider? Another bowl of soup before you leave?"

"We'll take some with us," said Angela.

"Don't be silly. You can eat it right here."

"We have to leave." Angela stood up so emphatically her chair fell over.

"Wait a while," said the woman, "and I'll prepare something." But she did not move toward the kitchen and Nicholos observed in her manner the nervousness of one who is losing control of a situation. "Please sit down again. My husband would never forgive me if. . . ."

"If you let us get away?"

"My dear, you don't understand." The woman's back was now braced against the door. She was again urging them to wait, to rest, but her voice was running down like an old victrola.

"Stand aside!" ordered Angela. She had passed round the table and was confronting the woman. "There's a bounty, isn't there, if you turn us in? An extra food ration? Where is your husband? Has he gone for the police?"

Nicholos was on his feet now.

"Don't you see, this is the only way?" The woman's voice was urgent, pleading. "We're thinking of your best interests, too. You'll die out there."

"That's our business," said Angela. "Get out of the way!"

Red and determined, the large woman barred the door.

Nicholos glanced wildly around for another exit. The windows were high and shuttered for winter. A second door was nailed fast, and it did not yield when he hurled himself against it. If only he had his father's strength, it would have burst from its hinges.

"Out of the way," screamed Angela, "or I'll kill you!"

She snatched a heavy-bladed butcher's knife from a peg on the wall but the woman did not budge. Her fingers groped along the wall and found the handle of a broom.

Nicholos grabbed for the knife as the broom came up, but Angela was too quick for both of them. Sudden as the closing of a steel trap, the knife shot forward into the woman's body at the spot where the bodice tied about her waist.

"For the love of God, Angela!" whispered Nicholos. He held her now, too late.

There was no outcry. The woman's cheeks bellowed out like those of a wind cherub. The broom fell, and her hands spread wide as though in benediction. Then she slid to the floor with her back propped against the door.

With a great sob Angela tore herself from Nicholos' arms. He had no will left to hold her. Dumbly he watched her ransack the cupboards for food, which she swept into a basket. Then she ordered him to open the door. He pushed against it so that the woman settled backward, half inside the house, half out. Her eyes looked up at him in astonishment. The terrible teeth were bared, in a wordless exchange that would stay with him for the rest of his life, and her lips seemed splashed with lipstick that had not been there before.

They were free and running. Behind them a bubbling voice rose and fell like wind in the rafters. A chained dog lashed to and fro in the yard. There was no one about to set it upon them except a startled child who flattened against the wall as they ran past.

Pursuit was certain to be swift and vengeful. At the fold, Angela routed the children out. "The police are after us. Hurry!" That was sufficient explanation.

Nicholos lifted Aphrodite in his arms, but Angela stopped him. "Do you want to kill her?" She turned her back on them both. By the way that she stood, he thought she must be crying, but she made no sound. Worst of all, she was right, but he couldn't desert the child without an explanation, without offering her some hope. He tried to make her understand. "You'll be staying, Aphrodite, where it's warm." Her arms did not release him, and he had to use all his strength to free himself. "You're too sick to go with us, but people are coming who can make you well. Just rest, and soon they'll be here." The little girl did not reply, but the

151

look she gave him would haunt him as surely as the surprise in the dying woman's eyes.

Outside the fold, Angela had gathered several of the youngest children together. She seemed to be lecturing to them, and when Nicholos arrived she told him they had decided to stay with Aphrodite. He opened his mouth to protest, but Angela wasn't listening. To each she gave a rough embrace, a word of encouragement. "People are coming who will feed you and take you home. . . ." Then she caught Nicholos by the arm and pulled him along with frantic energy.

Quickly they overtook the Metaxas twins, who were already driving the other children toward the wooded foothills. Angela resumed the lead, Nicholos his position in the rear where he could watch for strays. Besides himself, twelve remained, fleeing through an alien land.

On the edge of the first trees stood an empty farmhouse. Its broken door, swinging on a bent hinge, waved them on their way. Before plunging into the forest Nicholos scanned the waste behind. Seeing no sign of pursuit, he too lost himself among the skeleton trees.

The forest was dead. Even the pines were bare and black from fire. Many had fallen, so that the smaller children tripped over them. Regardless, Angela maintained a frantic pace, and Nicholos was forced to carry the weakest in turn. Gradually his legs became leaden, then rubbery and fire seemed to scorch his lungs. He seemed to be pushing through waist-deep waters, slowly and more slowly, until he had to call out to Angela in a rasping voice.

Among the scorched spires of the forest they finally rested. Nicholos sat with both hands over his nose and mouth to warm his breath on its way down. "Waste and void, waste

152

and void," his father would have said but, as Nicholos very well knew, this was only the beginning of the wild country.

Angela urged them on again until they reached the living forest. This soon thinned, giving way to rock, and a rocky mountain trail. Toward evening they discovered a shelter, a stone cairn with a door which a hermit must have built long ago. While light remained Angela wanted to go on, but Nicholos could carry the little ones no farther, and they sat in the path and refused to budge. Angela damned them helplessly, then grudgingly admitted that they might find nothing better for miles.

"It's sturdy," said Nicholos, glancing inside. "It'll keep out the wind. And the wolves."

Angela shrugged. The fury and the fear had gone out of her.

The Metaxas twins shambled inside and threw themselves down. Nicholos and Angela propelled the others after them, and none too soon. Before the door was sealed, Nicholos heard the first lone evening call, followed by an answering wail, then a sorrowful chorus. The wolf pack was with them still.

He found a wooden bolt on the door and drove it fast into its stone niche. Angela had set the basket of food down where the children could help themselves, but he wasn't hungry. She was not eating either, but sat rigidly with her back against the rough wall. Her eyes were open and unblinking. He sat down beside her and tried to think of something to say, but could not. Close as they were, it was as though something physical and dangerous lay between them, real as a coiled snake. If he could only talk of it, perhaps it would vanish.

"Was there nothing else you could have done, Angela?"

he said finally, knowing what he said was not the right thing, and knowing too that it had to be said. "Did you have to use the knife?"

As though to preserve the barrier, Angela stared silently at the ceiling.

"Look at me, Angela!"

Her dark gaze turned full upon him. "Why talk about it, Nicholos? What's the use?" Again she looked away. "What else could I have done? Tell me . . . you have enough conscience for both of us."

"I'm not trying to blame you, Angela. Why can't you look at me? Is it because you feel guilty?"

"Listen, you're as much to blame as I am. Whatever I have to do because of this mob is your fault. . . . If I'm bad, it's because I have to be. You fixed things right at the start so none of us had a chance."

These accusations he accepted fully. Whatever became of the children they had abandoned, it was his fault. Whatever became of them all . . . even the stabbing might not have happened had he not brought the children. Yet Angela had wielded the knife with intent to kill, and for Nicholos there was no more unpardonable sin. Though he avowed a certain responsibility for the deed, he knew he would never have used the knife. To a deep and involuntary part of him that fatal weapon seemed like the carrier of a loathsome disease which the person he most loved had contracted.

The March night had fallen. As the wind filtered through the chinks in the stone, it became bitter cold. The children crowded together, whispering about fires, about home. Only Angela and Nicholos sat apart, separate and subdued. Over and over he reviewed the scene in the farmhouse. He wanted to find some excuse for what Angela had done. Finding none, he offered her a chunk of bread from the emptying basket, and she accepted it with a faint smile.

"Have you ever seen such a dark night?"

"Black as pitch," she said, thoughtfully. "No moon. No stars."

"Only the wolves."

Nicholos sensed that her black mood had passed, and there was no use probing further. He would only bring it back. Better to plan for tomorrow. "How long do you think it will take us to get to Monastir?" he asked.

"Not long, with the. . . ." In midsentence Angela stopped, sprang to her feet, seemed to flutter out of control like a bird shot in flight. She rushed to the empty basket, felt wildly through it. "Oh . . . oh, isn't this funny!" she laughed hysterically. "I've lost it! I've lost my compass! I left it on the table. I left it with her!"

The compass had meant so little to Nicholos that he did not at first feel the importance of its loss, but Angela rocked forward with her face in her hands. "Don't, Angela," he whispered. He wanted to smooth her hair gently, but could not. There was still something between them—or in himself —that prevented it. "Angela, it doesn't matter. We know Monastir is north of here, and they say it's so high and strange-looking you can't miss it. Don't worry. Once we find Monastir, all we have to do is follow the road. You said so yourself."

"Oh Nicholos, I feel lost. . . . I feel lost forever."

He could only guess how much her past assurance had depended on the compass. It had steered them all the first night, and its loss was disturbing. But to suffer more over a bit of metal and glass than for a woman murdered, for infants

155

abandoned in the snow, seemed to Nicholos completely unnatural.

"Eat and rest," he told her. "Tomorrow we'll find Monastir."

He led her over to the others and persuaded her to lie down in the nest of children. There it was warm.

At first Nicholos only dipped below the surface of sleep. He tried to summon up the comforting dreams of his childhood before the war, but nightmares came instead. His mother was calling him, and when he found her she held a knife. She was covered with blood. Then she was dead, and he placed beside her body a white bowl of clear water and a fresh towel, so that Saint Michael, the black angel who takes the souls of Christian dead, might bathe his sword and dry it. Finally he plunged deep beneath all dreaming, to awaken refreshed. Angela still slept beside him, but shivered as she had done the night before.

He started to rouse her, but drew back his hand. Softly he went to the door, removed the bolt, and stepped out to see what the day was like. A veiled sun was coming up angrily behind coppery shreds of cloud. Snow was in the air, but his concern for the weather was quickly banished at the sight of the door which had been bolted during the night. It was scored by claws. He tried to convince himself the marks were old, but on the ground outside the door were fresh prints, gigantic prints, like those of his childhood terrors. Such enormous paws could belong to but one creature, whose deeds had earned for him a legendary name: the white wolf of Monastir. The sight prickled the hairs at the back of Nicholos' neck, and he was afraid with a deadly fear. Why had he not heard the creature during the night, this silent wolf? Had the wind been high? It seemed more than wolves that ringed them. A mysterious force of positive evil was engulfing the world.

Splinters from the door lay in the snow, yet the wood had held. Now it was broad daylight and the threat had passed, but night would come again. He would never have the fortitude of Saint Francis, who had said, "Come hither, brother wolf." Neither did he possess his father's strength to grapple barehanded with the beasts.

There was no food for breakfast, so they left at once. Nicholos stood in the doorway and checked them off. Twelve, counting Angela. How quickly eight had been lost. He placed his back against the door itself, hoping that none would notice the marks, and none did.

Ahead of them, the sky had taken on the color of tarnished brass. The landscape had a prehistoric look, and seemed to grow more threatening as the slope became steeper. All about the wide stony pastures swept down from one ledge of rock to another. Here and there the ground fell away beneath their feet, forcing them to swing wide, losing distance and direction as well.

Under the faint sun, the clouds cast changing shadows so that the mountains themselves appeared to change, and Nicholos began to share Angela's concern for the compass. The more they climbed, the higher the mountains seemed to tower into the sky. What confidence he had that they were approaching Monastir was no reasoned judgment, but simply a deep sense of rightness. Soon they must see it, the dread mountain about which tales were told to frighten children.

They were advancing into a land without human domicile, where pagan gods were said to lurk in exile. This land was traversed only by shepherds and their flocks, who toured its ravines like wandering patches of mist. All was cold and silent, and Nicholos knew that Angela was afraid of the heights. "I can't feel the cold up here because I've become part of it," she said during a brief rest. Nicholos loved the mountains. He respected them for their careless cruelty. Someday he would climb to the highest peak, though he knew a man could not dwell there long.

Toward dusk, Angela stopped on the top of a ridge and the children clustered around her. She was pointing ahead. When Nicholos reached them, he saw a mountain in the distance. Its rounded point thrust into a steely cloud in a frozen land where life had long since ended, or had never begun.

That pyramid was unmistakable, as though forged by savage man for a savage god. "You see," he told Angela, "we're on the right track after all." Without a compass they had found the way to Monastir.

11

They passed the night in a shallow cave furnished with straw by shepherds for a summer home. Nicholos lay near the entrance with a rock in his hand, and in his sleep became his own father, hurling stones against imaginary wolves. From these battles he repeatedly awakened to hear only the soft breathing of his companions. While it was still night, he knew he would sleep no more. He had agreed to waken Angela so that they might scout the approaches to Monastir, but in the moonlight she looked strangely like their mother; no, older, older than their mother could ever have become.

Alone, Nicholos went outside. He knelt and faced the brightening sky behind the bladed peaks. He spoke not to God, but directly to the mountains. Then he set out along the narrow trail. When the snow crust broke underfoot, he cursed it for slowing him down. Where the stony ridges were free of snow, he made better time, but the stones cut into the rubber soles of his shoes. It wasn't the pain he minded, but the knowledge that with the shoes his feet were failing, and he cursed them too.

The path led through a landscape of freakish stone pillars, scarred by wind, blackened by lightning, draped round with whorls of snow. Only the glowering peak of Monastir assured him he was still on earth.

At last the trail curved slowly to an open ridge, then fell away to a chasm below. Beyond it reared the pyramid of Monastir, as final as a white marble tombstone. The gap he had come so far to see was flooded with mist. It was like staring into a bottomless lake, and he would have to squander precious minutes of daylight while the sun rose and thrust down straws of light to suck up the mist.

Nicholos sat down and massaged his feet. Each one pulsed like a separate heart, but at least they had feeling. They were not turning black.

Gradually the scene unveiled itself, ridge by ridge. There was the river Dragor flashing silver, the roofs of Bitolj like red stairs climbing toward open pastures, and finally the road itself, slashing through the mountain gap. The road home. For fifty miles there was no other real road and he had found it. All that remained was to carry the news back to Angela and the children. Joyfully he leaped to his feet, then hesitated when the nervous winking of a tiny light told him that someone near the road was signaling with a mirror. If they were Yugoslavs, the gap was useless to them. If Greeks, they were as good as home.

Nicholos made his way to another vantage point near the brink, sheltered by a low mound of snow-covered rocks. From here he could see not only the signal light but black specks moving on the road. There were men and mules and a tiny flapping flag which Nicholos tried to persuade himself was Greek. He closed his eyes for a moment to rest them from the glare. Looking again, he made out three figures ascending a narrow path. Baggy coat and patched trousers identified them unmistakably as Andarte!

Nicholos dared not move, but waited for them to pass not twenty-five yards below. He could hear their voices plainly, but it was the cigarette that informed him. The way it was held, the way the match was struck. With the curling away of the smoke he recognized the vulpine features and the scarred brow. . . . "Thanos!" he whispered, as though the name might exorcize the apparition.

Nicholos crouched there with his hands on a round boulder. He felt it shift, ready to roll. One boulder would pick up others, gathering a wave of snow and thundering down upon the trail below in a suffocating, bone-shattering avalanche. It required a single push on his part, and Thanos would vanish. Two other men would vanish as well, and he would go away more guilty than Angela. He would go away three times damned to hell. His hands curled into fists, and he waited until Thanos disappeared. This time it was all right. He had controlled his impulse, but Nicholos told himself they must never come face to face again.

The trip back became a reckless, lung-burning flight in which Nicholos felt himself closely pursued. Sometimes he thought he heard shouts or howls, but he did not look back. The road through the gap was closed to them all. Thanos straddled the way like a devouring colossus. Better the highest mountains, the deepest snows. . . .

Blundering around a sharp curve in the trail, Nicholos found the path barred by an animal. He continued, thinking it was a dog, then saw it was a wolf. Too young to be really dangerous, it held its ground with bristling back, and eyes that caught the light like corrupt drops of water. Nicholos' surprise turned to fear, not so much of this small beast but of all that wolves had represented throughout his life. They were death's ally, and though this one seemed lost and starving, he feared it. Nicholos retreated down the trail. He was a coward and told himself so aloud, but he could not shame his legs into another confrontation. It was only by taking a tortuous detour that he got under way again. At least no one had witnessed his behavior and he had suffered no physical damage, but what if it had been night? What if the wolf had been the white one?

His tortured feet were about to give out when he reached the dark entrance to the cave. The children huddled in the pale sun and stared at him with dull eyes, too cold and hungry to be curious.

"We've heard wolves," announced Yamris.

Angela emerged from the cave and demanded, "Nicholos! Why did you do that? You promised to wake me."

For the moment Nicholos was too breathless to reply, nor was he sure how much of his adventure he ought to reveal.

"Well, what did you discover?" Her voice was brittle. Her face still looked strange, with the sharp bones standing out and the eyes sunken. Probably a mirror would disclose the identical story about himself. And the children? He could not look closely into their faces any more.

"I found out that my feet are bad . . . that my stomach's empty."

"Nicholos!"

He closed his eyes. The night before he had given his ration to Christo, and he felt the lack of it now.

"Stop the crow talk. Get to the point," his sister commanded.

Nicholos steadied himself. "All right . . . this is what

162

happened." He told Angela everything, except for the detail she would have found most interesting. It was dishonest not to mention Thanos, but he knew she was still attracted by that strange, violent man. The bond between them might be stronger than before. After all, they were both killers now.

"We'll have to choose another route, then, won't we?" said Angela.

"We've no choice."

"I remember some paths crossing this one back a little," she said.

"So do I," he replied, approaching the necessary decision cautiously. Until the loss of the compass, he had left the prerogative of command clearly up to Angela. Now her indecision left a vacuum he felt inadequate to fill. "You're the smart one," he assured her. "It's up to you."

"Don't put too much confidence in me."

"I've always trusted you completely. You know that," he said, and until the last twenty-four hours it had been true.

"Well, don't. It's up to both of us, so listen carefully and tell me if you disagree. We must be about twelve kilometers from Monastir, but whether it's north or west of us, it's hard to tell without a compass. Anyway, we can't be far from the Greek border. As long as we can't go directly to the road, we want to head south. Does that sound logical?" Nicholos nodded his accord. "We'll have to take the best trail we can find, so long as it's not toward Monastir. Eventually we should get to Greece. With any luck we'll find a town. Maybe Florina."

While Angela talked, they had walked back along the trail. They stood now at a juncture of paths, and Angela said, "All right. . . . Which way do you think is best?"

Nicholos' judgment was based on the wind, the direction

of the shadows, the slope of the land. Instinctively he made his choice.

"You'd take the mountain trail, would you? Maybe you're right, but think a minute."

Angela unfolded her map, locating various mountains, with little studied movements of her hands, isolating one fact after another. "It seems to me the mule path is more southerly, and if it snows we wouldn't be up so high. . . . You don't think I know what I'm talking about, do you?"

"I didn't say that."

"But that's how you feel. What if I took the mule path?" she asked. "Would you go the other way?"

"You know the answer, Angela. We have to stay together."

"The truth is, Nicholos, I don't know any more. Without the compass, I'm guessing, and we can't afford to be wrong. We'll kill them all."

He offered no reply, and they started back. He expected her to resolve the disagreement in her favor, but all she said during the walk was "All right, Nicholos." And when they returned with the children, she did not lead them down the mule path, but chose his way, the mountain trail. Nicholos was astonished. For once she had listened to him, though he knew if he had been faced with the final decision, he would have weakened and given in to her judgment.

They had been walking for more than an hour when he saw Angela stop. The others drew up beside her, crowding about an object in the path. Peering over the shoulders of the children, Nicholos realized an animal had been horribly butchered. Not even wolves could so completely dismember a body.

"Did a bomb fall on it?" he asked.

164

"It must have stepped on a mine," said Angela. "Here's a hole."

Nicholos had never eaten mule meat, but he carried what scraps he could and loaded the children with the rest. Since it was frozen solid, they would have to thaw what they wanted to eat by holding it under their clothes.

Though Nicholos welcomed the food, its condition came as a warning. He remembered the Andarte burying mines on the road from Serifos, and felt sure that one mine indicated the presence of others. They would have to find another trail. Higher up the slope he located a goat path, narrow and rough, where they were more exposed to the wind which rose steadily in the afternoon.

The wind would not let the snow rest, but blew icy crystals along the surface, stinging their sallow cheeks into caricatures of health. The little figures plodding ahead of him scarcely looked like children any more. They were more like elderly gnomes with ugly faces, but they were his now, and he loved them. He loved them so much that he decided angels were not beautiful, but gray and ugly too.

Angela's voice struck at them, shrill and cutting as the icy gale. "You'll be left behind if you don't move faster. Wolves will get you." But Nicholos knew their spirits were failing. They wanted to go home, to lie down where it was warm. One of the smallest did lie down. "It's going to snow. You'll be buried alive. Only wolves will dig you up." The little boy was motionless, and Angela walked away. Either she intended to frighten him, or she didn't care. Nicholos was not sure any more, but he pulled the child to his feet and kept him going with an arm under his shoulders. Christo rode like a lead anchor on his back, and his body felt ready to snap.

The landscape was weird, pitiless. Nicholos recognized it as the abode of the hermit, the eagle, and the storm. He was dimly aware of Angela passing up and down the ragged line, haranguing them, propping them up on rubbery legs. When they failed entirely, it was his job to persuade them that hunger and cold and snow in their shoes could be borne a little longer.

He shouted after the Metaxas twins to watch for stragglers, but they appeared not to hear him in the wind. It made no difference. So many refused to go further that Angela called a halt behind an outcropping of rock.

"Nicholos, we can't spend the night here."

"But they've got to rest." He made the children form a tight circle for warmth. He told them to eat. Though much of the meat was still frozen, they gnawed and quarreled over the chunks like a pack of weary cubs.

"The snow won't hold off much longer," said Angela.

"You can see the trail's heading down from here. We'll find shelter soon."

"If I only had the compass. . . ."

Nicholos had never seen her so completely without confidence, and he said vaguely, "We've got to have faith that things will turn out."

"Oh, that's comforting, Nicholos! Things always turn out one way or the other, but just suppose those brats can't be budged? Faith or no faith, we aren't getting them all home."

"We will, because we have to. . . . Don't you see that, Angela?" This was not simply to encourage her. Nicholos believed it absolutely.

Angela did not appear to listen. Her hand was upturned,

166

fingers spread. "It's starting," she said. "The snow will keep coming . . . there isn't a thing we can do about it."

"Except keep moving."

Angela laughed until the laughter became a sob. She cried quite openly and without hiding her face. Nicholos watched her, then closed his eyes to see where his strength lay. When she was quiet, he told her, "Angela, it's time to go. I'll get the others started. You take the lead with me last, so no one gets left."

"You amaze me, do you know that?" she said. "All right. . . . I can last another hour if you can."

Angela put her left hand to her forehead, just touching it with her fingertips. She rose, swaying. In the white whirl of this trackless wilderness, she looked to Nicholos like a lost soul. Then she started off with her head up. Whatever hell she might be bound for, a part of him would be with her.

Nicholos walked at the rear of the column. His rubber shoes were worn through, and his feet with their thick horny soles did not hurt any more. They did not seem to exist. He had eaten none of the meat, but had given his share to Christo, and his stomach felt hollow. Not painfully so, but with a lack of sensation he mistrusted. One hand steadied Christo, the other crept under his coat to a place over the center of his body where the hunger lay. Though he recognized these symptoms as dangerous, his mind moved apart in a world of its own, where he was as sure as ever that all would be well.

That they had managed this far was a miracle of endurance. More was expected, much more, or the white wolf, the enemy of his life, of all their lives, would take them. He would come out of the driving snow and Nicholos would have to fight with him.

Half blinded, Nicholos could no longer see Angela. There were only those atoms of humanity that clung to him; to his hands, to his shoulders. It seemed that Christo could not be alone upon his back. There were hundreds there, crushing him down, but he must keep moving. Not one could be left behind. Not one could be abandoned until they reached Serifos. He could see them, pouring down the last green grassy slopes. There would be flowers, and sheep lifting their heads as they went by. There would be his father ringing the chapel bell. That was how it had to end, not here on this barren mountain. As long as he kept going, there was nothing to fear. It would end with the Judas bell ringing out for joy. The happy bell. . . . He felt at peace, at peace. . . . He could see them so clearly now, his young knights and squires, his tattered angels. The veils of snow became the banners and the butterflies, fluttering up in brilliant clouds. They were approaching the holy land. They would find peace, the shepherd's peace, the peace of green pastures. . . .

Angela was shaking him. Nicholos was dimly conscious that he had fallen down and did not want to be disturbed. Angela shouted at him, slapped his cheek. "Come along, Saint Francis! Don't die out here in the cold. You can make it! We've found shelter, a chapel, a whole town, and plenty of wood for a fire. Come on. . . . Get your feet going! . . . That's right, left foot, right foot. . . ."

12

His first awareness was the slow pulse above his ears and the infinite hiss of falling snow. On opening his eyes, he had no idea where he was. Above him a heaven filled with sooty angels suggested that he was dead, but his stomach was too empty, his body too wracked for Paradise. He turned his head. Along the walls were fiends with forked tails roasting lambs over spits. Under this scene appeared the legend, "Lord, have mercy upon us." It was a chapel, so worn and neglected he could almost hear the worms gnawing the wooden icons of the saints. These icons were blackened with candle smoke, and about them hung votive offerings: beaten silver replicas of feet, eyes, hands, and legs.

Slowly he became conscious of the innumerable pains and numbnesses that composed his body. Gingerly he tested himself and was abruptly aware of what seemed to be a super-natural hand placed in his own. From the bench where he lay, one hand hung down out of sight, and there was a living weight upon the palm. He did not move for fear that whatever it was would fasten on his fingers. Slowly he rolled his eyes until he saw a sleek coat and a bristling whip of a tail. He drew his hand away violently, and the rat skittered across the floor. Other living shadows froze or darted into hiding places. For a moment he was alone. His companions lay on the floor asleep; not naturally so, not as children who have listened to a fairy story and been tucked in bed, but as broken dolls that have been carelessly strewn.

On the dusty floor were trails made by the bodies of rats. Their dwellings must spread beneath the chapel like the intricate roots of an immense tree. Below him was a forest of tiny roots in which rats ran in place of sap. And there would be vermin without legs; spiders, worms, the whole insect kingdom. He felt a certain kinship with these crawling creatures. Perhaps one day when things were better, they would not have to kill one another to survive. Maybe then all living beings would be friends and call one another brother and mean it, as Saint Francis had.

"Hello. How do you feel?"

It was Angela.

"I'm sorry I let you down," he said. "I almost ruined everything."

"What do you expect? Giving your food to Christo, then carrying him on your back . . . and look at your feet, Nicholos."

"Did you get us in here by yourself?" he asked her.

"Lias and Yamris helped. I practically had to club them over the head, but they helped. It wasn't far. You couldn't have been fifty meters from the door when you fell."

"We'd all be dead except for you. You saved the lot of us." He wondered if the saving of a dozen lives could make up for the deliberate taking of one.

"You make it sound like a miracle."

170

"There are miracle workers," he told her.

"Yes," she replied. "A good many of them are here." She wandered down the wall, idly touching the icons. "Look at the plaster. Everything's rotten, or wormeaten, or undermined by rats. . . . Just like us, Nicholos."

She laughed, and he did not like the giddy sound of it.

"Is there any food left?" he asked.

"Bones. The rats didn't leave us much during the night. Here's a thick juicy prayer book. That's all there is except the rats and the saints."

"I wonder where we are?"

"I wouldn't know any more. If you were right, we ought to be in Greece."

"At least we're clear of Monastir and the Andarte. Didn't you say there was a village here? Is it inhabited?"

"I don't know. Half these frontier towns have been burned out by the Andarte, and I guess most of the rest have been abandoned."

"Even if the place is deserted there may be food in the houses," said Nicholos.

The children were waking up, examining their surroundings with the listless expressions Nicholos had come to associate with refugees.

"What do you think? Shall we try to go on?" he asked.

"I've always known you weren't practical, Nicholos, but I didn't think you were crazy, too. There's a blizzard outside."

"At least we can take a look at the village," said Nicholos.

"Then I'll go with the twins." Angela's fierce energy seemed to be burning her body up, and to Nicholos she looked as if there wasn't much of it left.

171

"I can make it alone," he told her.

"Not with feet like that."

"Forget my feet. You're better at cheering up the young ones. They need you."

"Listen, Nicholos, it's not only the snow. I guess you were too exhausted to hear anything during the night. . . . Wolves, Nicholos! They seemed to be right outside, crashing against the door. They must be wild with hunger."

So the wolves were here, too. Perhaps it was the first timid pack from Albania, magnified and made savage by the fearful weather. Perhaps they were the wolves that had pursued him since childhood, the wolves about which shepherds made up tales. Such phantom wolves, the shepherds said, dug in cemeteries after a funeral. "To eat," one had told him, but another had said, "No, to carry off souls to hell."

"Did the others hear?" he asked.

"I don't think so."

Small consolation. On a day as dark as this, the creatures were very likely still about. "I don't think any one of us had better go out alone," he decided. "We'll go in a bunch, with weapons, if we can find any."

"If only we had a gun," said Angela.

"The candlesticks are solid brass," replied Nicholos.

Armed with these and accompanied by the Metaxas twins, they went out into a snarling world lit faintly by a distant and invisible sun. Behind them the chapel doors were bolted.

Barely discernible was a white Christmas-card town. On drawing closer Nicholos saw its beauty vanish as the snow covering failed to conceal broken windows, unhinged doors, the blackened trace of flames. Not a living thing was in sight except a lean dog which appeared around a corner, then leaped quickly back upon seeing them. Nicholos had never seen a town so desolate, and yet he had a queer feeling about the place, as though he had been here before.

"This isn't a town, it's a cemetery," said Angela with her hands cupped to Nicholos' ear. Yamris, too, had a message. He and Lias were sure it was the place they had burned with the Andarte. They didn't remember the name.

"Psarada!" said Nicholos. He knew it now. "Then we're near Florina."

"And near Monastir, too," said Angela. "We must have swung in a half-circle."

"The guns and the ammunition are hidden up there . . . somewhere. I'd like to get my hands on them," said Yamris.

"You couldn't get far in this storm."

"When it stops."

"When it stops, we'll destroy them," said Nicholos.

"After I get what I want." Yamris' tone as usual bore a challenge, but Nicholos let it pass. When the time came, he knew what to do about the guns which had been laid away for the attack on Florina. For the moment, they must deal with Psarada, for Psarada was dead and they were still alive. Nicholos found a loose shutter and tore it free from its hinges. Inside a doorway he found a pile of posters printed on brown butcher's paper. They would do to start a fire. Except for this, and a few pieces of wooden furniture the twins had dragged into the street, the town was bare of fuel. Food was even scarcer. Nicholos recognized the bakery by a sign that creaked in the wind, and under the counter he found some hardened lumps of dough. In another house, a smoked leg of mutton, suspended from the rafters by a cord, had escaped the rats. Nicholos cut it down and stuffed his pockets with a pile of rags he found in a corner. With them he might be able to bind his feet.

They kept on from house to house, hoping for a miracle: a cellar crammed with provisions, heaps of woolen blankets, boots. They found no such things, and had almost reached the end of the street when an incredible sight held them speechless. A rift in the storm clouds had sent down a long spear of light, and the entire village became visible. At the end of the street an old crone with white rivery hair appeared, broom in hand. She was sweeping snow from a doorstep.

Angela exclaimed, "Is that creature real? What can she be doing here?"

Real or otherwise, they needed help from any source. Before the snow closed over, Nicholos trudged down to the old woman, who heard him at the last and turned, crouching, to fix him with squinted eyes. Under the white hair her face was multicolored: cheeks yellow and flabby, with red patches where tiny veins lay near the surface, nose pink with greenish blotches, like spoiled ham.

"You . . . boy!" Like an ancient cricket, she shuffled as if about to jump. "You . . . come here to me."

With blue-veined hands she explored his face, feature by feature, as though she could not believe he was real. "So, they're coming back at last. Didn't think you'd find me still here, did you?" The old woman laughed cleverly. "Thought I'd be dead." She scratched the back of one hand with the nails of the other. "Where are the rest of you? Speak up . . . don't lie to me."

"At the chapel," said Nicholos.

"You were all fools to leave. I told you you'd come

174

crawling back, didn't I?" Her eyes were so close to Nicholos that he could see flecks of blood in them.

The snow was falling again. Nicholos tried to pull free, but the grip on his shoulder tightened. "I've got to get back . . . to the chapel," he told her. "Could you tell me first how far it is to Florina?"

"You're a shepherd, boy. You know as well as I do. Yes, I know you all right. You're one of the brats who steal figs from my tree. Don't lie to me! I'll take the hide off you." Nicholos asked her if she had any food to spare. "Little sneak thief! Don't lie to me. Where are the others? Sneaking behind. . . . I see them!" She glared fiercely around.

As she did so, Nicholos broke away. He took high leaping steps through the snow while the crone shrieked after him. Finally the snow muffled her cries.

"Did you find out anything?" asked Angela. "What about food?"

Nicholos shook his head.

"Why not?"

Still breathing hard, he tapped one finger against his forehead. The old woman had been alone too long.

On the way back, Nicholos saw the dog again. He was not sure this time that it was a dog. He did not trust the way it watched from the alley, the way it moved off, hunched and stiff-legged. He remembered, too, what he had heard of shepherd dogs gone wild in the Grammos Mountains. They had become as dangerous as the wolves.

Inside the chapel, the children had been busy. Nicholos noticed a collection of votive candle stubs. Christo and another little boy were dragging a wooden icon from its pedestal.

"We aren't burning holy things," Nicholos told them.

175

Carefully, so as not to fracture the old wood, he replaced the painting of the saint. He was right, of course, but the naked stare that Christo gave him almost made him feel that he was wrong.

All afternoon the snow fell. The wind moaned around the chapel and he seemed to hear in its voice the howling of wolves. Abruptly and without warning came an awesome silence everywhere, inside and out.

"It's stopped. I'm going to have a look," said Angela.

Together they climbed the belfry stairs and shoved open the trap door. The bell that hung there was not as old and heavy as the one in Serifos. A boy could lift it, but he knew that his father would have needed help in raising the Judas bell.

In the bitter cold, the snow was settling. As veil after veil of it fell away, the bleak terrain emerged.

"It will snow again before morning," said Nicholos.

They waited as the horizon withdrew. The first slopes became visible, the hillside where weapons were concealed in a cave, the upper crags, and finally, as though gliding toward them, a monstrous shape revealed itself. The shadow of the mountain fell over them. They were in the blackness of it, towering, brooding, pagan Monastir.

Like some terrible magnet it had drawn them back. They were nearer now to the Andarte than they had been before, nearer to Thanos. Nicholos glanced at Angela, as though by some sixth sense she might know.

"What would you do if Thanos knocked at the door right now?" he asked.

"Why talk nonsense, Nicholos?"

"Suppose he did?"

"With arms loaded with groceries? I'd throw open the door. I'd kiss him, and I'd eat . . . oh, how I'd eat!"

She was supporting herself with both hands on the belfry rail and her shoulders sagged forward.

"But what if he came like us, with nothing?"

"Nicholos, we've wasted a whole day. We're no nearer home than we were yesterday."

"At least we're in Greece."

"But where in Greece?"

"Florina isn't far. It's a city. We'll be all right once we get to Florina."

"Once we get to Florina! Oh, Nicholos, you are crazy. With those kids sitting down in the snow . . . without a compass . . . with no food inside us. . . . We'll die, Nicholos."

Tears had begun to pour down her cheeks and for a terrible instant he seemed to see himself in her dissolving eyes. If only he could reach into them and save Angela from drowning.

"Don't, Angela. . . . It's not that bad. We may have to go a little farther, that's all."

"None of us can go another step. Nicholos, I'm afraid."

"I can give you courage," he told her.

"I don't want any. I want to sleep and be warm. Put courage into the others and leave me alone."

"Listen, Angela, we're all right for tonight. Tomorrow, if it's still snowing, I'll look for that old woman. She must have food to spare."

"If the storm keeps up, we'll have to take it whether she's willing or not."

"There won't be any stealing." Nicholos was quickly on the defensive.

"I don't give a damn about you and your conscience."

Angela's brief flash of temper cheered him, but she was too tired to keep it up. The rancor quickly departed from her voice. "Look, there it goes over the rail," she said, trying to laugh at his bafflement. "Can't you see it? It's our argument. It ran off."

The wind was rising again, and with it came the snow. Monastir gradually withdrew and the storm enclosed the chapel. "Let's go down," said Nicholos. "It's warmer there. . . . Angela, take my hand."

When they reached the chapel, they found the children surrounding the old woman with the white hair, who was haranguing them about stolen figs. While she talked, Nicholos allotted scraps of cheese and dough. He did not offer any to her. When the others ate, she took a dry crust from under her sweater. He found himself watching her suspiciously, greedily, wondering what else she had concealed at her house. Probably very little. As he watched, she crumbled the hard bread into pellets for her gums to suck.

Over the chapel hung a blackness that was heavier than the storm, and only the patched walls and their mean fire kept it out. Angela withdrew to a corner. Nicholos could not eat at all until she did. He took her a ball of dough which he had moistened in melted snow.

"Angela, you must eat."

She looked away, hiding her face. "There isn't any use eating," she said bitterly. Isolating herself further, she pressed one hand against the side of her face as though she had a toothache. This withdrawal he attributed to her guilt over the murder. If it compared at all to his feeling after the death of Stavro, then her sufferings must be extreme. He felt reassured to think her capable of such remorse. If only he could persuade himself that her crime did not matter, but it

178

did. It always would. He offered food to her lips but they remained tight shut. He was becoming his sister's keeper, and he did not know how to save her. He did not know what would happen to all of them if she did not rally. Needing a moment to collect his thoughts, he limped to a dark corner of the chapel, but not even here was there any privacy. Children followed him, whining for food and warmth. He explained that their supplies must be rationed, but they wanted a big fire. Let tomorrow take care of itself.

"We may still be here," he cautioned them. "Then, if we find more wood, we will have a bigger fire. And more food, perhaps. Now rest."

Christo asked if they might eat the rats.

"Human beings don't eat rats," he told them.

The rats moved restlessly. They could be seen all about, gathering like clumps of dust in the light, gliding through the shadows, disappearing.

"Wait until tomorrow. If you're cold, move close to the fire. Eat slowly like the old woman. Pretend you have no teeth."

They sat by the fire, in its very ashes, but they had teeth and they ate quickly. Soon there was utter silence except for the old woman who was sucking at the insides of her cheeks where the last tidbits of bread were lodged.

"You can see we are starving," Nicholos said to her. "Have you any food at home . . . for us?"

The crone tittered wickedly, and the tip of her nose nearly touched the tip of her chin. "Not for wicked boys who steal figs." Then she sighed, and when she spoke again it was the old theme of her missing people.

"Are you very old?" Christo asked her.

"Very old. Yes."

"Will you die soon?"

"Winter is a dreadful time of year to die," she said.

"Will you die in the springtime?" persisted the little boy.

Nicholos tried to hush him, but the old woman, with a clarity she had not displayed before said, yes, she supposed that might happen. Her face was beaming with pleasure. "I haven't had a conversation in I don't know how long. You're a nice little boy." She produced another pellet of bread from inside her sweater and gave it to Christo. "Now I'm going home where I belong. I'll come tomorrow when the rest of my people return."

"Don't go out in the dark," said Nicholos. "Stay here with us." But she walked stiffly toward the door. "You'll lose your way . . . there may be wolves."

"You can't keep me here. You're not my people." Her wild eyes fixed him crazily. Her hand fastened on the door.

"You're old," he told her. "You'll get lost."

"I'm old, and my life is nearly over."

She shuffled out into the night, and Nicholos closed the door and bolted it. The door was strong still, with its brass hinges. It would keep anything outside except the cold. The shrieking wind sounded so much like a human voice that Nicholos pressed his ear to the door. There it seemed more like a musical instrument in torment. What a place for an old woman, for anyone, outside that door. Against his body it rattled. It seemed to open and he leaned against it. Outside, like the black waves of an evil sea, he heard the night crashing around them. The entire world seemed threatened by a terrible flood of evil, rising to swamp them all.

Nicholos returned to Angela, sat beside her, and told her about the old woman. He tried to discuss plans, but Angela was not ready. "I love you, Nicholos," she whispered, trying to control the tremor of her voice. "I want you to know that no matter what happens. . . . I have a feeling I'll never. . . ."

"Hush. . . . Go to sleep."

"Talk to me a little while."

"What shall I say, Angela?"

"Anything. Say a prayer, if you like."

"I can say 'Our Father.' Shall I say that one?" Angela did not answer, so he began slowly. It seemed a good prayer for one who trusted God.

"You believe God watches over you, don't you, Nicholos? Nobody watches over me. Nobody except you. Isn't that strange? I'm not a good person like you. Remember, a long time ago I said you'd help me do whatever I really wanted? Even if it was wrong? I still believe that, Nicholos."

It was the murder that made her say things, thought Nicholas. He could only guess at the burden of guilt she bore. As long as she felt remorse, her soul might be saved, and she was his beloved sister still. He remembered a story, taught to him by his mother. It told of an angel who had received hospitality from a good man and afterward had strangled the man's newborn son. On the surface this seemed a terrible crime, but the angel knew more than man could know. The child would have grown up to murder his parents. Such a tale could not excuse Angela, but it seemed somehow to free him from the need to condemn her himself. Judgment remained to God.

"We'll be all right," he assured her. "We'll all be fine." Gradually the haggard look left her face. She became tranquil, as if after a long and terrible effort she had finally made peace with herself. Presently she turned toward the wall. If she cried, there was no sound, and after a while he knew that she slept. He got up to make the last arrangements before trying to sleep. Very little food or wood remained. He would

181

have to guard them both if they were to last, and he put the remains of the smoked mutton in the sleeve of his jacket and placed the jacket over the wood. He made a bed of them, and for a pillow he arranged the last few posters. The twins were watching him with sullen eyes and he pretended to be reading one of the posters. Some of the words caught his eye and he began to struggle with the meaning, but the printing was bad and he had never been skillful with letters.

> People of Greece: Hear us. The torch of War has been flung into our midst by the Anglo-American Imperialists. They have infected our Motherland with Gurkha dwarfs who sate their cannibalist appetites on the brains of our Children. They bomb our homes. We do not ask you, whose Ancestors were suckled by the running rivers of Heroic acts, to shed your blood with us. We ask of you only this: Food when we are starving, Shelter from the cold, the Denial of all succor to our Enemy and the unquestioned Right to take and protect Your Children so that they will not no longer fall before the Sword of the Anglo-American Imperialists. . . .

Many of the words were too big for him and what he did understand seemed ungrammatical or untrue. No Greek he knew would have written such a thing. No Greek he knew had ever met an Anglo-American, or a dwarf, for that matter, and yet the authors of this poster presumed to change a way of life about which they seemed misinformed. But such speculations tired him out and he placed the poster with the others behind his head.

Nicholos lay on his back. Above in the guttering shadows little fox-faced bats were coming to life, while outside the storm roared and shook the chapel. Borne on the tumult, he seemed to hear the voices of wolves.

182

13

Outside it was still snowing. Nicholos could tell by the sound of the wind. What would happen were it never to cease? He had wished for that once, and in a cowardly corner of his being he almost wished for it again. Then he pulled himself erect. He had not yet admitted that nothing remained but to die.

Christo slept beside him, smiling like a cherub. Funny how his mother used to say a person's sleeping expression was a mirror of the soul. Perhaps it would be better then if none of them awakened, but already Christo was stirring. His expression changed and it was obvious to Nicholos that soft slumber had given way to a consciousness of the world's injustice. Soon they were all awake, and Nicholos divided the last hoarded scraps of mutton on a bench. They did not fight over it, but consumed the few crumbs quietly with an intensity approaching ferocity.

Then Yamris spoke of the old woman. He and Lias were sure that her home was full of wood and blankets, her dirt cellar packed with olive oil and pickled lamb. They meant to pay her a call; politely, Yamris said, but if she refused them. . . . In his hand was a brass candlestick.

"Oh, no . . . we're not going to have anything like that," Nicholos told him.

"Watch out, Nicholos," said Yamris. "We aren't starving to death because you tell us to."

"I'll find food," Nicholos promised, without the slightest idea of how he could do so.

Yamris measured him up and down, from his rag-wrapped feet to his steady eyes. Silently Nicholos stared him down, and Yamris rolled the butt of his candlestick in the dust. "My brother and I. . . ." he began, but a cry from Angela cut him short. She had opened the chapel door and had seen something in the snow. Nicholos ran to her, with Yamris close behind.

In a welter of snow-softened tracks, Nicholos saw half-buried rags of clothing, all that remained of the last inhabitant of Psarada.

"All right, what do you say now?" demanded Yamris.

"About the old woman's place," added Lias.

The pair faced him, and he knew it would be dangerous to thwart them. Nor did it matter now. "Go ahead," he told them wearily. They would have felled him with the candlesticks had he said otherwise. "But bring back what you find."

The twins left immediately. Christo started to follow, but Nicholos held him back. He could not bear to see his favorite associate with such savages. "I'm going!" Christo insisted and managed to wriggle free. Angela caught him. He set his teeth in her hand and she hit him, hard. Christo slunk away inside the chapel, and Nicholos reproached her.

"You almost broke his jaw!"

184

Angela shrugged. "You wanted Christo stopped, didn't you? You're the one who was wrong for not letting him go."

"We'll soon be as bad as they are."

"He's frightened. They all are. They have to be controlled any way at all, or they'll be at each other's throats. Sometimes force is the only way."

"They have to follow us of their own free will. They've got to have faith, and we're the only ones who can give it to them." As the world about him fell in ruins, Nicholos found himself more and more resorting to his father's dogmas to prop it up again.

"I'm not arguing that," said Angela. "It's cold. Come inside. Sit close to me."

"Did you hear Yamris out there?"

"No, but I know him. He's an animal. But when it's a matter of survival, we're all animals, and you've got to accept that if you want to get home alive."

"If that's true," said Nicholos, "we'd all become Andarte. . . . Or wolves."

"Listen, 'Father,' " she began sarcastically. "No, let's not start that again. . . . I think the snow's letting up, don't you? When it does, we'll have to move on. Without food, we can't stay here."

"They may bring some back."

"Don't fool yourself. If there is any, they'll devour it on the spot."

She was right. The twins returned empty-handed. They said the house was empty, but their truculent manner convinced Nicholos their bellies were full.

The day wore on, cold and hostile now. Nicholos made frequent trips to the door. Outside the snow fell intermittently in large flakes. Tomorrow they would start out again for Florina, without a trail or a compass. They had no choice. He went from one child to another giving encouragement, trying to determine how much strength each had left.

Toward evening he climbed alone to the bell tower. The night was coming on sharp and clear. The moon was bright; the eye in God's face, his mother had called it. Spreading out below the chapel he could clearly make out the town of Psarada. He studied it carefully, as he had on the day before the attack. That day seemed long ago, part of another lifetime, yet the thatched windbreaks behind which the Andarte had concealed themselves still stood. There were the orchards, like black talons against the moonlit snow. He could even see the grove of carobs where he had stood that morning, and behind them must be the cave full of explosives.

Far below in the valley, so faint it might have been a trick of vision, he saw a fluttering light which he took to be the Andarte's fires. He scanned the horizon for other lights, for a glow which might be Florina, but saw none. All was serene and deadly and utterly still except for shadows that weaved in an intricate pattern directly below. His relentless enemies, the wolves, were encircling the chapel, apparently seeking a breach in its wall.

When a wild shriek came from beneath his feet, Nicholos assumed that such a breach had been found. Recklessly he flung himself down the ladder, only to see the children excitedly clustering around the entrance to the altar room. Using their candlesticks as crowbars, Lias and Yamris were prying up the tiled floor. Angela was helping them and at first Nicholos thought the trio had gone mad.

"What are they doing?" he asked Christo.

"Hunting."

"Hunting what?"

"Rats . . . to eat."

It was true. Yamris stood back from the exposed nest. This time it was empty. "We'll get them. We aren't giving up," Yamris told the children, and Nicholos knew they would hunt again. Soon the children would no longer need him. They would hear only Yamris.

As though responsive to a silent command, they went on tearing at the tiles and it seemed as though they already had another leader, an invisible one that had come to squat among them by the fire.

Nicholos stood up, demanding attention. "Listen, everyone. I want all of you to get a good night's sleep. In the morning we're leaving for Florina. It will be a hard trip, and you'll need all your strength, but we'll get there. In a couple of days we'll be home."

They stared at him as though he were a stranger, speaking in a foreign tongue. Angela got up. "Nicholos," she said, "this is something we have to discuss."

"I'm discussing it now," he told her.

"Come on. We'd better be alone," she said, and the grip she fastened on his wrist was strong and emphatic.

They moved to the altar room and the twins followed. Nicholos told them to go away, but they crouched on their hams and listened.

"What makes you so sure we can get through tomorrow?" asked Angela. "We have no compass, no mules to carry us if we get tired. We can only guess where Florina is." He knew she was a realist who constantly weighed the facts, while in his own brain the facts caused only confusion. He had ceased wrestling with them long ago.

"God will not abandon us. He told me so."

Angela stared at him with a flicker of scorn. "You were dreaming."

187

"Yes, of course. That is how God speaks to us."

"He won't help us here. What would God be doing in this hellish place? Please, Nicholos. . . . This has nothing to do with God, but at last I know what has to be done."

"Tell me, then."

"Well, the snow's stopped and we can't last much longer here without food."

"Not another day."

"And we can't go very far, either," she said. "Not with all these children."

"Then you and I will go, and bring back help."

"Suppose we didn't make it? What would become of them here alone?"

Nicholos was beginning to feel trapped.

"I know how much you want to go home, Nicholos. But think of the dangers. If we escape snowslides and the wolves, we'll only get lost, and freeze to death."

"No matter what you say, I'm sure I can find the way, Angela."

"Have you really looked at those kids lately? We've dragged them, and carried them on our backs until we couldn't go on. Do you think they're grateful? Nicholos, they only want to stay alive and they'd as soon kill us as follow us. Even if all of us wanted to go on, we'd die before we got near Florina."

Angela was being silly. She was frightened, and so she was trying to frighten him. She could talk all she liked about facts, but there was a certainty growing inside him, sure as the pull of a magnet, that would guide them. He had only to respond to its impulse and the rest would follow. If only he could explain to her, but she was still speaking and he forced himself to listen.

"This is what we have to do, and I don't like it any better than you will."

Suddenly Nicholos knew what was coming.

"You mean surrender to the Andarte."

"I don't know any other way. . . . Nicholos, listen: the Andarte have food."

"Maybe this time they'll let us join them," said Yamris.

"That would be better than dying," said Angela. "And we wouldn't be there forever. Nicholos, try to understand." Her hands were in motion, as if she hoped to smooth the troubled air between them. "I've seen it coming. Ever since we lost the compass. Don't despise me. Over and over again I've called myself a traitor, but there isn't any other way."

"Angela, the children depend on you to lead them. They want to go home."

"Ask them, Nicholos. Ask them. They just want to stay alive. You're the only one who thinks about home any more. They hardly remember home."

Could he have been wrong all along? No, he had to be right. What Angela was asking of him was against his nature, against God. "If I do as you say, I'll go to hell," he said.

"Do you seriously believe in hell?" she asked scornfully.

"Of course I do. And Father? Don't you think he believes?"

"In sulphur and brimstone, and devils with pointed tails."

"Not like that, but in remembering always what you've done. Just feeling forever that you've failed. Angela, we've got to keep going."

Home lay to the south. Instinct would show him the way. They would take the others with them, willing or not. Even perishing in the snow seemed preferable to a life of savagery among the Andarte. "Besides," he said, in a voice

189

that sounded loud and high, "we can't go down to the Andarte, with Thanos there. Believe me, I'm sure of the way home. I always have been."

"How do you know?"

"I just know the way. Except for the mines in the road, we would have been all right before."

"But how do you know he's there?"

"Thanos? I saw him."

"Why didn't you tell me before?"

"What difference would it have made?"

She did not answer, but said softly to herself, "So Thanos is there too."

Nicholos also thought aloud. "He would kill us," he said. He did not really believe Thanos would kill Angela, but as far as he was concerned it amounted to the same thing.

Up to this point the twins had not intruded. Now Yamris spoke out. "There is another way," he said. "What if we had a couple of mules and some food? Maybe a compass, some guns. What about Florina then?"

"Marvelous," said Angela, sarcastically. "And why not a magic carpet while you're at it?"

Yamris seemed unabashed. "Suppose you do go down to the Andarte, Angela, and you tell them there are children up here too sick to be moved. You can get a couple of them to come with mules, can't you?"

"Go on," she said.

"Meanwhile, Lias and I will try to get a couple of guns from the cave. Even with the snow that shouldn't take long, and when you get back we'll be waiting out of sight for the Andarte to come. How does that sound?"

"You mean murder them?" Nicholos shouted. He would rather surrender than allow them to kill, and in this he was confident of Angela's support.

"What about it, Angela?" asked Yamris, as thought Nicholos were not even in the room.

"If I were sure you wouldn't turn coward at the last," she replied.

Nicholos was astounded. To him it was wrong even to contemplate such a deed. "For God's sake, no! I won't let you do that."

"No?" replied Angela. To Nicholos, her face looked carved from white stone, and her voice had a cold finality as she explained that it was because of him that they could not surrender, that Yamris' plan was the only sensible alternative.

"Angela, for the love of God! You've already murdered one person. Don't. . . ."

At his words a change came over Angela. She began to shake visibly, and her hands opened and shut, opened and shut. Her voice, coming from between clenched teeth, was cold with hatred. "Go to hell, Nicholos! You go straight to hell!" She kept on saying this over and over until he hit her, and he heard her still cursing him as he bolted from the room through the crowd of startled children and up the ladder into the bell tower.

Here he was alone, more alone than he had ever been in his life. Angela was against him now. They all were, yet in his abandonment he felt a new freedom. For the first time he could act without consulting anyone. Like his father, he would place his body and his soul between the others and their murderous designs. He would have to begin by destroying the guns and ammunition. All along this was what he had intended. The only difference now was that he would have to do it sooner and alone.

14

Nicholos did not want to see Angela again that night. He would not risk being delayed by her persuasions as he had been delayed so long ago when his lamb was lost. He stayed in the bell tower as long as he heard sounds from below. The cold found its way into his clothes, into his bones. When all seemed dark and silent he scanned the night for signs of wolves, and for the last time impressed on his memory the landmarks along the trail he would take. Then he went down into the chapel. In his pocket he gripped a handful of wooden matches, and no one challenged him as he secured a burning stick from the fire. Quietly he eased open the great door, pushing the stick ahead of him through the opening. More than the Andarte or the winter cold, he feared the wolves. Though there had been no sign of them from the tower, he expected at any moment to see their gathering shadows, their eyes, and with the chapel door against his back he said a prayer to Saint Francis of Assisi who had faced wolves without fear. Then he stepped away from his shelter.

A dry wind was singing over the snow. If wolves were

watching, they did not show themselves. The moon and the snow combined in a kind of dream daylight, clearly illuminating the trail. The snow was shallow behind the windscreens and the low stone walls, and he moved upward in a zigzag path toward the dark patch of carobs. On the ridge the snow had blown thin and the crust was hard.

He did not need the torch for light, but it was his sole protection and he kept it with him. When the wind extinguished the flame, he bore it still as a club. No wolves appeared in the walled fields, or in the grove of carobs, or at the cave entrance which suddenly yawned before him like an open grave. In the sheltered mouth of the cave he tried to rekindle his torch, but failed. He went on, striking one match after another, until he came to the supplies, crates of explosives and loosely stacked arms, sufficient to obliterate Florina and her citizens for generations to come. There was enough loose cardboard and rough pine to get a fire started, and when the flame seemed certain to expand into a blaze, Nicholos ran.

He burst from the cave. Heedless of the winding path he crashed straight through the carob grove and slid headlong down the icy slope to stop waist-deep in a snow drift. Battering through the snow, he ran again until an incandescent flame opened the sky and a rush of hot wind threw him flat. Then came the explosion, cracking and whistling. In a fearful confusion of the elements, sounds came from the earth and out of the air, and went on reverberating across the valley, against the far mountains. With terrible internal rumblings, snow began to shift, one slide triggering another as Nicholos lay awaiting the deadly inhalation of frozen dust that would drown his lungs in ice water. The sounds diminished, the echoes died into silence. The serene night seemed to collect itself. A wolf howled dolefully, became a chorus.

Nicholos picked himself up and went on toward the faintly glowing chapel. They would have heard the uproar, and he would have to explain. They would be angry at first, but in their hearts they would know he had done the right thing.

Before the chapel doors he saw a shadow, so slender and rigid he knew at once who it was.

"Come inside, Angela. Don't you hear the wolves?"

"You fool! You stupid, stupid fool!" She spat the words.

He wasn't going to argue. There was no point to it now, and the explosion had taken all the anger out of him. Toward Angela he felt almost paternal. He tried to put his arm around her to guide her inside, but she pulled back.

"We'll have this out right here," she said. "It's been your fault from the start. Everything! And now this! All because of your interference!"

"Angela, listen. I know what I'm doing," he began patiently. "Maybe killing that woman was an accident, but this. . . . You wouldn't be able to go through with it."

"I would kill her again if I had to."

"And Thanos? Suppose he had come with the mules. Would you let Yamris kill him?"

"Yes. I would kill Thanos myself."

"You're lying," he told her.

"Nicholos, you don't know me at all. If it were the only way I could stay alive, I would kill even you. I would regret it forever, but when I die the whole world dies as well. That's how I feel."

She had said such things before, but he had not been able to believe them. Now she had killed, was willing to do so again, and the brutality this indicated seemed suddenly verified by the stony face confronting him. That face no longer belonged to the Angela of his own creation, but to an imperfect stranger beyond his power to save or condemn.

He drew a deep, unsteady breath. "What do you intend to do?"

"I don't want to talk to you any more, Nicholos. . . . I can't bear it."

"Come inside. You'll think more clearly in the morning."

"I can't! That horrible chapel!" There was a brittle quality to her voice, as if at any moment the speaker might shatter into fragments.

"You can't leave tonight. You heard the wolves."

"Nicholos. . . ." She seemed about to surrender, but it was like the game on the cemetery wall which she had to win or would not play. "Nicholos, try not to hate me."

Hate! He could feel anger, jealousy, even disgust for his sister, but never hatred. The old Angela he would always love. This stranger he could not hate even though she stood in his way. She would simply have to step aside.

"I'll bring the Andarte back with me, Nicholos. You will hate me for that, too."

"Tomorrow you may change your mind," he told her. "Come inside now."

As he turned toward the chapel, the windows flared with light as though the entire place were on fire.

"They're cold. They must be burning the icons," she said apathetically.

"Not the saints! Angela, you've got to help me!" But she stood looking off into the dark.

The light inside was blinding. All the sacred icons

195

blazed in one great conflagration. The children crowded close, on their knees before it, palms extended. The roaring fire painted their pale cheeks while deep in its heart the ancient icons slumbered, their metal faces like the golden death masks of Mycaenean kings. Blue and purple sparks shot up, and Nicholos seemed to see shapes dancing there, animal shapes, and the figures of the apostles. Christ himself lived for an instant in the flames. Then Nicholos was furiously kicking at the fire, but he was too late to save the saints, very nearly too late to save himself. Without warning Yamris was on him, and Lias, too. A candlestick struck him on the cheek, and he sank to his knees. As he struggled to rise, spitting blood on the floor, he saw Christo advancing toward him, a smoking stick of wood in his hand. Though the distance between them was no more than an outstretched arm, thousands of years seemed to separate them. The child's face was bestial. The stick was raised, but something of the old bond must have remained, for as Nicholos waited the small face seemed to fold upon itself with crying.

Nicholos picked himself up and sat on a stone bench. A gash on his forehead felt sticky and warm, and the rags that wrapped his feet showed crimson patches. Neither hurt him as much as the attack itself, particularly Christo's part in it. If he ever tampered with their fire again, Nicholos felt they would tear him to pieces.

Through half-closed eyes he watched them returning to their pyre. They were building it up again. Saints had been transformed into blackened wood, and presently the fire would die. Why should he risk his life to save such a pack of animals? Why should he not set out alone for the peaceful pastures about Serifos? He was weary of their faces, for behind them he saw the faces of beasts. Still, he had to try to save Christo. . . . and Angela.

"Angela!" For a moment he had forgotten her. Fearing that she might have started for the Andarte camp, Nicholos stumbled to his feet and ran outside.

"Angela!" She had not moved a step. "Angela, I was afraid . . . you might have gone."

"Did they hurt you, Nicholos? Your face. . . ."

"Come inside, Angela."

"I never wanted them to come with us. If it weren't for them. . . ."

"Come inside. It's cold."

"Nicholos, I can't stand it in there . . . not any more. I'm going."

"Angela!" Unless he struck her to the ground he could not stop her now. He heard his own voice saying, "Angela, I've saved a little of the bread dough. . . ." and he felt his hand fumbling in his jacket pocket.

"Nicholos, you're the one who'll need that." She kissed him lightly on the cheek. They did not speak again, and he made no move as she started away from the chapel. He stood transfixed as the great pale night seemed slowly to swallow her up. She became so small, a tiny dark speck moving with dreadful slowness, which disappeared and came again, the merest particle against the white. Then there was nothing. It took him a moment to realize she had gone, perhaps forever. A great emptiness seemed to suck him down. This was worse than tears or pain or hunger.

15

"*Angela.*" Over and over he said her name. He might never see her again, even if he lived a thousand years. Yet behind his eyes he seemed to see her still, the old Angela, the Angela who had died. Asleep or awake, he would always see her as no one else ever would.

Over him towered the southern face of Monastir. Its immense gray silence weighed him down, pressing him into oblivion. With his arms held tight against his empty stomach, he knelt there rocking back and forward until his face almost touched the snow.

Above the soughing wind came another, more sinister sound, so like the wind he did not at first discern it. When he did, he did not care. Let them come. Presently he saw gray shadows moving against the snow. From their thrusting muzzles and their upcrooked tails he knew them, for they had traveled with him always.

The pack padded in a wide arc around the chapel, around the place where he knelt. Their eyes caught the firelight from the chapel and blinked back messages of

198

corruption. Gaunt and matted, their fangs gleamed as pale and ghostly as phosphorus. They had come at the right time, this silent army of death. He would welcome the deliverance they brought. His life, which seemed suddenly so empty, would soon be at an end, and as the wolves circled closer Nicholos never moved. He knelt with his head inclined forward, as resigned as a criminal awaiting the headsman's stroke.

In these last moments Nicholos prayed. He would have prayed for Angela, but she was dead; a fragment of his mind that had never been. So he prayed instead for the children, who because of his failure would surely die.

The beasts drew closer, narrowing their circle as though participating in some Satanic ritual. In the center his motionless figure seemed to puzzle them, as though an action on his part was necessary to complete the spell.

Nicholos could make out their bony faces. The malignant glimmer of their eyes turned upon him as they roved nearer, trailing their lank tails in the snow. In seconds he would be part of the turning circle. It would close over him. First one would slash at him, then all of them. Within the chapel, the children did not know about the wolves, but their world too would soon end. For this he was fully responsible. No one else would have brought them here to perish; not Angela, not anyone with common sense. In his own failure it seemed that God, too, had failed. But how could God fail? He wanted an answer before the wolves put an end to his thinking.

Slowly the memory of his father filled him. His father would not have left the children behind in prison. His father was like no other man on earth. To Nicholos he was the symbol of everything courageous and godly in the world.

What other man loved humanity so much that he would not avenge the killing of his beloved wife? What other man had the courage to stand alone against the Andarte? To attack wolves with his bare hands? The towering figure of Father Lanaras seemed to stand over him, offering strength, urging him not to give up.

Nicholos' fists clenched and his mouth hardened. He had questioned God! At times, he had questioned his father's laws, even broken them, but they had kept him from following Angela into the darkness. His father's laws! Here lay the answer. It was not that they had ever failed him, but that he was failing them.

Slowly Nicholos stood erect. He dared not run. His enemies were close on every side. They were what he had always feared. All that was savage, deadly, and evil in the world seemed distilled into these wolves. But even if he had held a weapon, he would not have killed these half-starved beasts. He could not hate them, for like the rest of the world they were driven by hunger. With his arms spread wide, Nicholos asked aloud what he should do, and the wolves seemed to listen.

There was silence all about. Nothing moved except one vast shadow, pale and ghostly as the moonlight. It advanced upon him across the snow and gradually materialized into a shaggy shape. Not so gigantic as he had imagined in nightmares, yet larger than life, it loomed before him; the white wolf of Monastir.

No more terrifying image could have confronted Nicholos, yet he did not falter or run. He seemed to feel his father's hand on his shoulder. He seemed to hear his father's voice. He took one forward step toward the waiting horror, and then another, and as he advanced he no longer felt afraid or confused.

He was almost upon the white wolf before it moved. Before his eyes, it appeared to fade and sink back into the moonlight without moving its limbs, as one might see a great stone sinking into the depths of the sea. Nicholos stood alone under the moon. The snowfield where the pack had circled was bare, silent except for the wind murmuring over the snow. "God's icy wind," he whispered aloud, and with his right hand made the sign of the cross in the air. He felt as though he were safe in God's great hand above a bottomless chasm.

The vision had been for Nicholos a promise and a covenant. He had survived for a reason, a purpose he must never betray. Alone, without food or guidance, he would lead the others home whether they wished to follow or not. They must leave before dawn, for even if Angela never reached the Andarte, they would have heard the explosion. They would be coming with first light. Nicholos did not think beyond this. He had not been born for reason and logic, but for faith. Now, he was filled with it, and confident in his own ability to push into the future no matter what the odds. Neither snow nor the mountain barriers would stop them.

He had imagined it all before. This was a beginning and not an end. The icy air seemed to soften in a rush of warm spring breeze. The distant hills looked green, and when they reached the valleys, butterflies would fly up around their feet. For years to come, peasants would make up songs about their march, about how a shepherd led them home. He had only to put heart into his companions. Filled with joy, Nicholos ran toward the chapel.

They were asleep when he arrived, clinging together for warmth, their pale faces smeared with soot, their hands still grasping candlesticks, yet in the glow of the fire they looked pathetically innocent. He felt strong and sure of himself. His first impulse was to wake them immediately, but they were young and tired and would have to travel far. For a few more hours he would let them sleep. He lay down beside Christo. There was no danger of his falling asleep. The tremulous memory of what had occurred outside kept him awake, and when the time came it would give him the courage to face them all.

Toward morning he passed among the children, whispering them all awake. When all were conscious, he spoke in a loud, clear voice. "Listen to me now. I have good news. Do as I tell you, and tonight we will sleep in Florina. Tomorrow, at home in our own beds."

As he had anticipated, Yamris shouldered roughly forward, followed by Lias. They carried their candlesticks.

"Where's Angela?" demanded Yamris.

"Gone."

"Where?"

"She is dead."

A look of doubt came into Yamris' face. He glanced uneasily at his brother.

"You killed her?"

Nicholos denied this, but clearly Yamris did not believe him. Nicholos would have erased such an ugly thought, but in his challenger's gaze he recognized a new respect. Respect for such a reason sickened him, but if it took a murderous reputation for the twins to accept his leadership, then let it stand.

He led them all outside before the sun had cleared the

heights. High up the mountain walls, icy glaciers streamed with brilliance like illuminated honeycombs, but around the chapel the world was blue and soft, warmed by the wind called the Notus, wafting up from Africa.

Nicholos ordered the twins to lead in Angela's place, and they obeyed him immediately. To the small ones he spoke more gently. "Not one of you is going to be left behind, but we must travel as fast as we can." When they were all spread out in single file, he took up his place at the rear.

For a few hours they seemed to be the only living beings in a trackless waste of snow and rock and stunted black trees. Then, as Psarada was about to pass from sight, Nicholos saw a chain of black dots moving in column toward the town.

He shouted at the twins to quicken their pace, but they were taking turns breaking a trail through the deep snow. They could do no better. He encouraged the others to sing, and for a while they chanted tunelessly. As the morning wore on the column lengthened and wavered and grew silent. Snow had got into their shoes, soaked through Nicholos' bandages. He felt his strength leaking away through those rotten rags. All of them needed a rest, but across the valley Nicholos could still see the chain of black dots moving closer. He began to count steps aloud for the children as Angela had done, and involuntarily looked around for her before he remembered.

Their only chance was to reach Florina before they were overtaken, but at each turning new expanses of snow unfurled below. Foothills and valleys still lay in blue shadow, and there was no sign of a town. Gradually the shadows withdrew, to be replaced by dazzling white. Otherwise the only change was in the pursuers, who were no longer dots, but clearly men.

With the warmth of midmorning, Nicholos became aware of the muttering barrage of sliding snow. The weight of fresh snow was pressing down on the high ridges, and the early thaw was eating away at the anchors which held it in place. Nicholos realized that there was a growing danger of avalanche. He knew that somewhere one small cornice might fall and roll, and begin a friction of rolling particles. In seconds it would bring the avalanche wind howling down upon them, and behind the wind, tons and tons of hissing snow.

If an avalanche came, it would be the end of them. Nicholos did not even attempt to set a course that would lessen their danger. The Andarte were too close for that. All he could do was to shout directions to the twins and keep the others moving. "They're feeling it now," he told himself aloud, "and God knows, so am I." If the children heard him talking like this, they would think he had lost his mind. They probably believed that already, and he began to sing once more. This time no one followed his lead. Perhaps they didn't care any more whether they got home to live in freedom for the rest of their lives or were held as slaves in a foreign land. To be caught would at least be an end to running. But as Nicholos' body weakened, his spirit became adamant. They had come too far, suffered too much, to fail.

The valley down which they were moving had narrowed rapidly. They were paralleling a river which was bridged here and there by layers of ice. The deep water moved sluggishly as though half-frozen, but with the thaw it was beginning to swell. Soon it would be foaming down the valley which other spring thaws had slashed like a saber cut through the mountains. As the banks steepened into a gorge, it became cold and dark. High up, sunlight shone on the snow cornices and on the ice which gleamed in rainbow tints. A tinkling hail of icicles and sifting snow fell about them from the warming cliffs.

The twins had stopped. "We don't dare go any further," said Yamris.

"You know they're right behind us, don't you?" said Nicholos. He did not know whether it was what he said, or what they thought had happened to Angela that made them go on again.

The deep whisper of the river grew more ominous as it rose slowly, devouring the crusts of ice that confined it. Where the banks were coated with spray, they had to slide on hands and knees with agonizing slowness. To control his impatience, Nicholos counted the seconds it took them to move by each difficult spot. Occasionally he looked back, but in the narrow defile he could see only a few hundred yards. If the Andarte came in sight at all, the chase would end in a matter of moments.

They had arrived at a particularly narrow portion of the gorge. Nicholos was helping Christo over an ice-glazed shelf of rock which jutted above the river when the canyon was filled with vibration like a great violin strumming. There followed a tearing noise and a gale of wind, then a hurtling roar which echoed into silence. Nicholos saw nothing, but somewhere ahead a mass of snow must have fallen into the gorge.

The twins turned back. From the hunched shoulders Nicholos guessed that they meant to give up. He scrambled forward to stop them before their panic infected the others. Though they all had a right to be terrified, Nicholos was vividly aware of being without fear himself. Since facing the white wolf, he had lost his capacity for being afraid.

"We'll be buried alive. We're quitting," said Yamris, his dark eyes froglike with fear.

"Take my hand," said Nicholas. "See? I'm not trembling. I'm not frightened, and you mustn't be either."

"They'll catch us whether we run or not," said Lias. "Look, you can see them coming!"

Nicholos jerked his head around. Not three hundred yards behind, he saw them. The Andarte were running hard.

Common sense told him to surrender, but his father would never surrender, not even now. If need be, his father would risk crossing that fragile bridge of ice. And without his father's great weight, his chance was that much greater. When he told the twins they were about to cross the river, Lias tried to lunge past him. Nicholos barred the way.

"You're crazy," the boy whimpered. "Let me go. You'll kill all of us!"

Where they stood, the river was spanned by a sheet of ice, but the swollen current was gnawing at it from below. At any moment the ice might splinter and vanish, but Nicholos did not hesitate. He felt himself acting upon an actual pact with God, and his confidence radiated from his face. Yamris stared at him, confused. "Hold my hand," Nicholos commanded. "And take your brother's hand. Everyone hurry." He formed them into a living chain of linked arms. The voices of the Andarte could be heard, shouting at them to stop, as Nicholos stepped out onto the fragile skin of ice that spanned the gorge. The surface was smooth, and the water moved beneath it like greased metal. Jagged cracks formed in the ice beneath their feet and shimmered out in all directions like frozen lightning.

Nicholos found himself repeating "Our Father. . . ." aloud. The others heard his words and said them too, and without a backward glance they passed safely over. On the bank they gathered about him.

Across the river, the Andarte had stopped. In the gloom of the canyon, their faces were indistinct, but when a solitary figure ventured onto the ice, Nicholos thought he recognized Angela. The bridge of ice was rapidly crumbling, and the figure stopped, seemed to waver. Then a hand was extended from the far shore. Thanos' hand? Nicholos could not tell, but the person on the ice caught at it and was drawn into the shadows. The Andarte started back the way they had come, and Nicholos guided his children in the opposite direction.

As the canyon walls gradually receded, the danger of avalanches should have ended, but the thunder of sliding snow continued intermittently, even grew louder as the high mountains fell away into hills. The explanation came jarringly, with a jagged cloud and the bright star of an explosion. They were walking into a battle. Nicholos felt that his companions would follow him anywhere now, but he knew, too, that their strength was giving out. For some time he had been carrying Christo on his back. The twins had followed his example, but by their unsteady progress he knew their legs would soon fail. If only they could locate the battery from which the shells were firing. It would be friendly, for the Andarte had no artillery.

"Stop!" he called. "We'll wait here and listen for the guns." The children did not try to form a group, but simply sank down where they were, twelve dark bundles strewn across the snow.

For a while it was enough to be still and to feel the warm glare on his face. Like lumpy sundials they sat there, with the shadows wheeling slowly around them and then stretching out across the snow which glistened for a while longer and became gradually infused with blue. The guns had not sounded again, and with the first chill breath of evening Nicholos roused himself. The afternoon was over, and night would bring fierce cold and the tracking wolves.

They should move on, but Nicholos knew not one of them could stagger a hundred yards, let alone the miles that still must separate them from Florina. Their only chance was to cling together in a tight circle for warmth and protection. He dragged the children together, and if his arms had been long enough he would have embraced them all.

There was nothing more he could do. He fought to stay awake, but as the darkness deepened his thoughts began to melt and slide to the edge of consciousness. Until morning, if morning were to come, he would have to leave it up to God.

16

Inside his head, he heard snow rolling down; or was it guns firing again? As he listened, it seemed to change into the low whine of a wolf, which grew into a terrible roar. In his dream, Roberto and his father appeared, and Roberto pointed a revolver at his face. Then it wasn't Roberto after all. It seemed to be Thanos.

"Where's Angela?" Nicholos said aloud.

A voice replied without making any sense. "They're alive, all right."

Another voice said, "Hey, which one of you's in charge?"

Nicholos tried to stand up. He pitched forward into the snow, real snow that was wet. The dream was over. The voices were real. "Here! I'm in charge," he called.

A Greek officer in a green coat nodded. "Any adults here? Any grown-ups?" The man gave a whistle when Nicholos told him they had been alone for days. "Any lost?" he asked.

"Not today."

The children watched silently. They looked at one

another with disbelief, and for the first time surrendered to tears. Their wailing spread from one to another.

The officer grinned at Nicholos cheerfully. His lean cheeks were blue with whiskers and the cold, and his eyes were narrow from squinting too long at the snow. "We'll lug you back with the plow," he said. "How many here?"

"Twelve," Nicholos told him.

"You look nearly dead. I guess we'll have to carry the lot of you," said the soldier, but Nicholos would not be helped. He took Christo by the hand and led him to the plow which sat on the snow like a great metallic cricket. Soldiers stood about it grinning, raising their automatic rifles as the children passed. In their friendly wondering laughter was the happiness of a promise kept, a victory won.

Nicholos rode in the cab beside the officer. It was hot over the engine and his eyes wanted to close. "We've been a long time without sleep," he apologized, and the soldier seemed to start from sleep himself. "Go ahead, close your eyes," he said. "It'll be some time before we get to Florina."

In spite of his exhaustion, Nicholos did not want to sleep. He needed to talk, to know what was going on. He began asking about the battle, and the soldier seemed to revive. "It's a butcher's business," he said with evident satisfaction. "These Andarte don't know when they're beaten. They've practically no arms or ammunition. One or two light cannon. Still, we've got to destory them if there's to be peace." So the war was really ending. That was all Nicholos wanted to hear. He soon lost interest in the details of slaughter, and as the soldier continued, he had to lock his jaw against the impulse to yawn. He was again fighting sleep, and gradually the heat from the engine overcame his resistance.

210

How his feet were cleaned and freshly bandaged, who undressed them all and put them between clean khaki blankets, Nicholos would never know. He slept that night like a corpse to which the warmth of life still vaguely clings, and not until morning did he find out they were safe in Florina.

They were to be returned to Serifos in an empty supply truck on its way to Athens for ammunition, but the truck would not start. By midday the attack was renewed, and the snowplows were busy clearing the roads. Serifos would have to wait.

From the edge of town a battery of howitzers began firing. It looked to Nicholos from their flash and report that they were firing harmless salutes, for the shells were invisible and vanished into the white waste of mountains without a trace. Somewhere they were falling effectively, for by late afternoon prisoners were marched through town. Hundreds passed in ragged overcoats, their hands pressed against the backs of their heads. They were young men mostly, with black eyes and hollow cheeks broken by cold and hunger and defeat. The roadside was cluttered with relics of their rout: haversacks split open, burst canteens, even a few rifles. There were women among them, too, indistinguishable from the men even in their willingness to fight and kill. They were without beauty, and, like their men, bound for the barren prison island of the Adriatic. Nicholos shut his eyes until his dizziness passed. He could not look at them any more for fear of seeing Angela.

Moving in the opposite direction he saw the Greek army: dark young men like the prisoners, but ruddy with health. Their new helmets rode low over their foreheads. With them tramped Evzones, so big they seemed grown from special soil. The Evzones swung their arms smartly and looked straight ahead, chanting the old war cry, "*Aera! Aera! The Evzones will pass. Aera! Aera!*" With the same cry the men of Marathon had smashed the Persians two thousand years before. The same men, the same war, it seemed to Nicholos.

At dusk he was called to the truck with the children of Serifos. They were going home. He knew they were proud of him now, and proud of themselves. The night was long, and the old truck waged a ceaseless jolting battle with the road. Above him, canvas flapped and cracked like gunfire and the air was thick with the smell of fuel, but he was warm and there was no more danger. Nicholos felt himself filled with a new repose. Within a few hours they would all be home. He would be with his father. He lay with one arm around Christo, breathing through a tunnel in the blankets. "God, dear God," he sighed, and would have added a thankful prayer had he not fallen asleep.

With the sunrise they arrived at Serifos. The driver helped them down where the village path branched away from the Athens road, and the truck rolled on south. A dawn mist lay everywhere. The houses of his village were softly outlined against the lightening sky. Home! Nicholos felt freedom and pure happiness buoying him up. He was like the eagles, circling slowly on their great wings, tilting to catch the wind.

Up the narrow road he led them. They would surprise the town. With the first signs of spring they were coming home. The village boys would be making wooden swallows to welcome the March winds. Soon flowers would be pushing through the stones. There would be butterflies, and they would not kill them or steal their wings. Strange how quiet the town seemed. No one had noticed them, not even a dog, and as they moved from house to house Nicholos began to see signs of desolation such as had not touched Serifos since the time of the German bombers. Windows without glass, burned rubbish in the streets; his head seemed to grow large and hollow with the sight of it, and blood hummed in his ears.

Scarcely a living soul was to be seen, and the few faces that looked from the windows were unfamiliar. Only when they were approaching the chapel itself did he hear voices. On turning the last corner, Nicholos stopped short. There before the chapel was a crowd of men, their wind-gnawed faces framed by uncut beards, their costumes dark and uniformly drab, and in the hands of each one a rifle. Nicholos could not have been more shocked had he seen a pack of wolves. He backed into the children, tried to push them all around the corner out of sight, but they flowed around him. They ran toward the chapel, throwing themselves upon the men.

It was only then that Nicholos realized they were not Andarte, but the men of Serifos, armed and battle-weary as he had never seen them before. There was Dimitrov the butcher, looking pale and worn with his left sleeve pinned up to his shoulder. There was Roberto, too, coming toward him, stopping, coming again faster.

Excitedly Nicholos ducked into his old friend's arms and out again, like a boxer from a clinch. Roberto held him at arm's length and stared as if he wasn't sure he was real. "Nicholos," he finally said. "You're supposed to be dead in the mountains, all of you."

"Where did you hear that?"

"The Red Cross. They picked up some children in Yugoslavia. They said the rest of you had disappeared."

"What's going on here?" asked Nicholas.

"We're going to war," replied Roberto. "We're all of us marching on Florina."

"But why?"

"Because of your father. He's like a fuse of black powder burning in all of us."

"My father wouldn't go to war. He's a man of God."

"Nicholos, listen." Suddenly Roberto looked very sad. "Your father's changed. He's a man of God on vacation now."

"Where is he? I want to see him."

"In the chapel, Nicholos. He'll want to see you."

Inside, the chapel was a shambles. Gun slits had been battered through the ancient walls, and littered about the holy place were rifles, sandbags, even a great coil of barbed wire. Only the Judas bell was the same, resting on the tiles onto which it had fallen months before.

Nothing moved.

"Father, are you here?" called Nicholos.

Finally from the sanctuary behind the altar Father Lanaras emerged. Clad like the others in the anonymous garb of the partisans, he looked emaciated, and yet to Nicholos that very emaciation seemed to magnify his physical strength. He was like a great bear, lean from hibernation. He folded Nicholos in his arms, and for a moment of painful joy Nicholos felt himself suffocated in the sweat-stained jacket. "Nicholos, thank God. . . . We'd given you up. . . . At first I didn't recognize you. . . ."

"You've changed too, Father."

"What about Angela? Is she safe?"

Nicholos could not answer at first. "Dead" was enough

214

for the others, but not for his father. "I don't know," he said finally. "She left us for them. . . . The Andarte."

He felt his father's body stiffen, but when the voice came it was level, without emotion. "Voluntarily, Nicholos?"

"Yes. The others followed me."

In fact the children who had found no relatives outside were clustering behind him in the chapel.

"You've done well, Nicholos," his father said. "You've grown up."

This was not as Nicholos had imagined their reunion. He had dreamed about it so long they seemed to be actors, trying hard but without much gift for acting. His father did not seem even to be trying now. He seemed far away already.

"Father, I saw Roberto outside. He said the men are going to Florina. He said you're leading them."

Outside the other men stamped, hawked and spat in the early morning damp. There were shouts for Father Lanaras to come out, only they called him *Lanaras* now.

"Is that all Roberto said?" asked Father Lanaras.

Nicholos was confused. He felt as though he were not addressing his father at all, but his father's ghost; his father's defeated ghost.

"He said you were a priest on vacation."

"Nicholos, I've written to the bishop. I'm a priest retired . . . for good." When Nicholos did not reply, he went on, agonizingly. "Nicholos, I've been alone here a long time, looking at this ruin of a chapel, at that bell lying there. At first I tried to put it back, but I couldn't alone. I couldn't even pray. All I could do was sweep the floor. When your mother was taken from us, I was filled up with fury, but I swept the floor then, too. This time the Andarte came back and it was make a stand in the chapel or die in the street. We held out for a day and a half until the troops came. You can see what's left."

"But Father, the chapel can be mended."

"I can't. . . ."

"I'll help you with the bell. . . . Christo and the others . . . they'll help."

"No one listens to bells any more, Nicholos."

"They will if it's rung loud enough."

"It isn't the bell or the chapel, Nicholos. Listen to me. When the battle was over I went into the streets. The mountains seemed nearer, more clearly defined. Do you know what I'm telling you?"

Nicholos did not understand. He put his arm around Christo. He saw that the others were listening, trying to comprehend, men and children together.

"There were friends of mine dead and dying, but I was lightheaded. I should have been horrified, but I had never felt more alive, as though I had been holding my breath too long and had suddenly let it out. When I looked up at the sky, the light was blinding, but I saw no sign of heaven there . . . or of God. It was then that I tore off my cassock. I threw it over Dimitrov, who was lying wounded. . . ." Here he seemed to run out of breath as though recovering from a desperate flight. "That night, I wrote to the bishop."

For Nicholos it was as though his father had gone mad. He was like a blind man leaping up a stairway that led nowhere. "But Father, why do you have to go now? The war's ending, and we're home." But they were not all home. Angela was not home.

"Nicholos, I persuaded the others to go. They've lost

216

children and their friends have been killed. They want revenge."

"You want revenge too."

"I know only one thing, Nicholos. I want my daughter." He took a terrible breath like a sob. Nicholos expected his father for once to give in to his emotions. He wanted him to, so that he might offer some consolation, but visibly Father Lanaras battled with himself. He stood more erect. "Nicholos, I can't delay here if there's to be any hope of finding her. . . . Will you come?"

"I'll stay," said Nicholos. He knew they would never find Angela, nor would they find the children who had disappeared in the trucks so long ago. They would find only the last few desperate Andarte. "We'll stay. I'll have to find a home for some of the children."

There was only one way for him now, and it was at once the hardest and the only possible way. Violence and warfare might drive evil back into the mountains for a time, but they could not destroy it, for violence and warfare bear evil with them. There remained his father's old way, infinitely slower, too demanding for most men. Even Saint Francis had failed to improve the world, as his father had failed in Serifos. But Saint Francis had set an example of faith and charity which seemed to Nicholos all a human being could do, until some far distant day when ordinary men would not have to be savages to survive. Perhaps then a man could look at a lamb as a lamb, not as an Easter dinner. Then a wolf could lead a snowbound man to safety, and men would speak one language and never betray one another. Then the white wolf would vanish from the world. If this were only a dream, it was still the one toward which the rest of his life would be directed.

217

His father was still speaking to him, but he did not answer. He went outside to call all his companions together, even those who had found their fathers. In the chapel doorway the men stepped aside, made way for him, as if they were afraid. When he had all his companions together, he told them, "Most of you have homes to go to. The rest of you may stay with me at my home." He put his arm around Christo and the child looked up at him with trust and admiration.

"What about you?" he said to the twins. "If you're not following my father, you can help me. I want to ring the bell so people will hear. I want to speak to them all.

The children looked at one another. They did not answer, and he turned away. Without looking back, he went to the Judas bell. It was heavy, but if need be he would raise it to the tower alone. He would ring the ancient bell for those who stayed, and for those who took the road to Florina. He would ring it for all to hear, but his first effort barely moved it across the tiles. Then he was lifting it easily. Eleven pairs of hands were helping him.